I0654861

William S. (William Sumner) Appleton

Early Wills Illustrating the Ancestry of Harriot Coffin

With Genealogical and Biographical Notes

William S. (William Sumner) Appleton

Early Wills Illustrating the Ancestry of Harriot Coffin
With Genealogical and Biographical Notes

ISBN/EAN: 9783337074265

Printed in Europe, USA, Canada, Australia, Japan

Cover: Foto ©Raphael Reischuk / pixelio.de

More available books at **www.hansebooks.com**

EARLY WILLS

ILLUSTRATING THE ANCESTRY

OF

HARRIOT COFFIN,

WITH

GENEALOGICAL AND BIOGRAPHICAL NOTES,

BY HER GRANDSON

WILLIAM S. APPLETON.

BOSTON:
PRESS OF DAVID CLAPP & SON.
1893.

WILLS.

IN the Name of God Amen the two & twentieth day of Decemb^r sixteene hundred sixty & eight I Edmond Greeneleife, being mindfull of my owne mortality an certainety of Death, & vncertainty of the Tyme & beeing desirose to settle things in order, beeing now in Good health & perfect memory doe make appoynt & Ordaine this to be my last will & testament in Manner & forme folowing, That is to say first and prinsipally, I give & bequeath my soule into the hands of my blessed redeemer the Lord Jesus who hath Dyed & gaue himselfe for mee, & his blood cleuseth from all Sinne & through his righteousnese I doe onely looke for Justification & saluation, and doe comit my Mortall body, after this Life is ended vnto the Dust from whence it was taken, there to be preserued, by the power of the faythfulnese of my Redeemer Jesus Christ, vntill the Resurection of the Just, and then to be raised vp by the same power to Imortality & Life, where I shall see him as he is, and shall euer be with him & in this fayth & hope I desier through his Grace & Assistance to liue & Dye in, & at last to be found of him in peace, Nextly my will is beeing according to Gods will reuealed in his word that we must pay what wee owe & Liue of the rest vnto whose rule the sons of men ought to frame there wills & actions therefore my mind & will is that my debts shall be truly and Justly payd to euery man to whome I shall be indebted, by my Executors heereafter named, And first I doe reuoke renounce frustrate & make void all wills by mee formerly made & declare & appoynt this to be my last will and testament Imprimis I giue vnto my sonne Stephen Greeneleife, and to my Daughter Browne Widdow, and to my Daughter Coffin to each of them twenty shillings apeice, Item I giue vnto my Grand child Elizabeth Hilton ten pounds, Item I giue to my Grand child Enoch

Greencleife fiue pounds, Item I giue to my Grandchild Sarah
Winslow fiue pounds if her father pay me the foure pounds he oweth
mee, Item I giue vnto my Eldest sons son James* Greencleife
twenty shillings & after my funerall Expences debts & Legacies are
Discharged, I giue & bequeath the rest of my Estate, vnto my son
Stephen Greencleife, and to my Daughter Elizabeth Browne, and to
my Daughter Judah Coffine, equally to be diuided amongst them and
their Children & further I desier & appoynt my son Stephen Greenleife & Tristram Coffine the Excecutors of this my will to see it
Executed & pformed as neere as the can & I farther intreat my
Cozens Thomas Moore Marriner to see to the pformance of this
my will, In Witnese whereof I haue set to my hand & seale this
twenty fifth Day of Decembr 1668.

Signed sealed published & Declared
to be my last will in prsence of vs   EDMOND
    George Ruggell   GRENLEFE & a seale
    John Ferniside.

When I maried my wife I kept her Grand Child as I best remember
3 yeare to Scooling Dyet & apparell & William Hill her son had a
bond of six pound a yeare whereof I Receiued no more then a barrell
of porke of 3lb : 0-0 of that 6-0-0 a yere he was to pay mee & I
sent to her son Ignatius Hill to the Barbados in Mackrell Sider &
bred & pease as much as come to twenty pound I neuer receaued one
penny of itt: his Aunt gaue to the three Brothers 50lb : a peice I
know not whether they receaued it or noe but I have not receiued
any pt of it.   Wittnes my hand
beside when I married my wife   EDMOND
she brought mee A siluer boule   GREENLEF   29. 5. 68.
a siluer porringer a siluer spon
she Lent or gaue them to her son
James Hill without my consent.
Proved 12 April 1671.

ANTHONY SOMERBY.

In the name of god, and with the assistance of his holy spirit, I
Anthony Somerby of Newbury in the County of Essex Newe
Ma being sencible of my owne weaknes & mortality, being through
gods mercy of Indifferent health of body & of perfect memory, doe
here make my last will & Testament, Comending my Soule into the
hands of my blessed Redeemer Jesus christ, and my body when it
shall desceaso this fraile life to be buryed in the burying place of
Newbury betweene my deare Relations my wife & son, In an assured
hope of a blessed Resurrection, And for my worldly goods which

---

* There is no other trace of this son, and perhaps the name should be Joseph.

god of his free mercy hath betrusted me with in this my pilgrimage I desire to dispose as followeth

Imp^r I give & bequeath to my Grandson Henry Somerby all my now dwelling house & barne & housing with the freehold of Comonage belonging to it, with Orchard & twenty eight acres of Arable & pasture land, adioynceing to the house with my portion of Salt marsh in Plumb Iland (except six acres which I reserue for his two brothers next Joseph Cokers land) & I also give him my six acres of Salt Marsh below Pine Iland all which I giue him dureing his naturall, and to his lawfull heires but if lawfull Issue faile then I giue it to his next brother prouided that he fulfill my will here expressed.

It. I giue to my Grandaughter Elizabeth Moody (besids what she haue had) twenty shillings in mony, and ten shillings to her son Daniel within one yeare after my descease.

Also I giue & bequeath vnto my Grandson Abiel Somerby the foure acre lot that was John Hutchins with the Orchard & freehold of Comonage belouging to it. And a parcell of arable land lying on the west of that I purchased of John Hutchins, bounded from about the midle of the said orchard fence on a strait lyne to the rocke on the brow of the hill & from the said Rocke on a straight lyne to the street fence being about three acres more or lesse the foure acre lot to come from the south west corner of the orchard fence, in the ancient bounds through the calfe pasture also I giue him three acres of Salt marsh in Plumb Iland & halfe the six acres I bought of Sollomon Keyes with my musquet sword & belt this I giue him dureing his naturall life & to his lawful heires but if lawfull Issue faile I giue it to his brother Anthony & the booke of Mr Dike on a good conscience.

Also I giue & bequeath vnto my Grandson Anthony Somerby my pasture land called the new pasture as it is fenced in to itselfe & six acres of Salt marsh that is three acres in Plumb Iland & three of that I bought of Sollomon Keyes, those two parcels of Salt marsh to be equally divided between Abiel & Anthony: and my ten acres of meadow in birchen meadowes to be equally divided between Henry Abiel & Anthony, This portion I giue to Anthony when he shalbee of the age of one and twenty yeares dureing his naturall life & to his lawful heirs but if lawfull Issue faile then the pasture to Henry & the meadow to Abiell also I giue him my bible & Mr Rogers seauen treatises & a Carbine & sword.

Also I appoint Henry to break vp two acres of land for Anthony.

Also I giue vnto each of my Grandaughters Abigail & Rebecca fifty pounds a peice to be paid in corne & cattle at the dayes of their marryag or in a twelue month after or at the age of one & twenty years or two & twenty.

Also I giue Elizabeth Morse a cow & two ewe sheep at the day of her marryage.

And wheras my Daughter in law had a hundred pounds allowed

her for the thirds of her husbands estate there is threescore pounds in her brother John Kellyes hands, And I appoint her that threescore pounds, and forty pounds more to be paid to her out of my Stocke by my executor with the goods that are in her Roome, And to haue liberty to dwel in the house without any molestation; Dureing her widdowhood her son Henry to find her firewood & to pay her six pounds yearly in Corne & prouisions And in Consideration of Henry paying my debts & legacyes and his mothers six pounds yearely I giue him all my booke & bill Debts & all my stocke & household goods vndisposed of And to have Abiels work vntill he be of the age of one & twenty years finding him meat drink & apparrell Also I giue to Mr Richardson twenty shillings in pay & to Elinar Davis twenty shillings in pay & to Richard Bartlet ten shillings & thirty shillings to the poore of Newbury

And hereby I appoint Henry Somerby my true & lawfull heire & sole executor of this my last will & testament

And Desire my trusty & well beloued freinds my brother Tristram Coffin & my Cousen Nathaniel Clark senr to be the ouerseers of my last will & testament Revokeing all former wills acknowledging this my last will & testament my debts & funerall being Discharged

January 22th 1685

As witness my hand & seale

owned & sealed before us   Anthony Somerby   Seal
   Augusten Steedman
   Willim Moffit
Proved 26 October 1686.

Richard Knight.

This 17th of Agust 1681

I Richard Knight of Newbery being now in helth and while my memory is good and know not how sudenly I may leaue this world and being desirous to set my outward estat that God hath given me in order acording to my Minde do Therfore ordain and make my last will and Testament as followeth.

First That when my time is com I commit my soule to god that gaue it and my body vnto the Earth to be buried to waite for my Reserection by my Lord Jesus Christ.

Secondly I give and bequeth vnto my Granchild John Keley my lot at the old toune joyning vnto Josep Elslys vpland and the oxcomon and ffive ackers of marish medow joyning vnto mr Sewales marrish land and Josep Elslys and by Thomas Heals. And Likwise five ackers of marrish land at Plom Iland joyning vnto my daughter Rebeca Somerbys land she had of me and by Capt Daniell Perces land on the south with all the apurtenances belonging to it : (erasure) all this land vnto the said John Keley to Inioy to him and his heiers for euer after his mother Sarah Keley and his ffather John

Kelleys decease but if my Granchild John Keley dy without anie child surviving of his body lawfully begotten : then the whole both vpland and medow to return vnto his brother Jonathan Keley and his heiers foreuer : but if John Keley do liue to Inioy it he shall pay vnto his Brother Jonathan ten pounds in Marchantabl corn or catell vnder 7 yer old and If Jonathan com to Inioy it he shall pay unto his sister Rebeca Keley ten pound in like pay.

Thirdly I giue vnto my Granchild Richard Keley my house and housing and barns and orchards and all the rest of my land both vpland and medow and pastures and comonag with his brother John to Inioy to him and his heires for euer after his mother Sara Keleys and his father John Kelys decease : and if Richard Keley dye withont a Child surviving of his body lawfully begoten Then the whole both housing barns and orchards and all the land before mentioned for Richard To Return vnto his brother Abiell Keley and his heirs for euer with the Comonag and privilids before mentioned : and Ife Richard Keley do liue to Inioy it he shall pay vnto abiell Keley twenty pounds in marchantabl corn or cattell or ife Abiell Keley do Inioy it he shall pay his sister Sara Keley twenty pounds.

4ᵗʰˡʸ Concerning my son in law Henry Jaquis and Ann his wif when they were maried I gaue them thirty ackers of vpland and medow and now I giue vnto him three pounds to be paid within three years after my decease and likwise I giue vnto Ann his wife fiue pounds to be paid within fiue years after my decease or before if my executors can well do it.

5ˡʸ I giue vnto my Granchildren Anthoney Mosse and Josep Mosse ten pounds apeec and vnto Elizabeth Mosse twenty pounds : the forty pounds to be paid within seven year after my decease or before if my Executors can well do it.

6ˡʸ Besid the medow and Cattell I gaue vnto my daughter Somerby when she married with Abiell Somerby : I do now Ingaig my executors to pay vnto my daughter Rebeca Somerby sixty pounds that I then promised within a yer and halfe after my decease.

7ᵗʰˡʸ I do now make my daughter Sara Keley and her husband John Keley my Executors and to Inioy all my housing and all my land both vpland and medow with all my Comonag and privilidges and ffences belonging to my land and with all my stock of Cattell and horse kine and sheep and swine and goods during their lives : and do Ingaig them by this psent to pay the fore mentioned Lygacies which is on hundred and eight pounds and within the time prefixt and my debts and Charg for my ffunerall and to my ouerseers for their pains and time expended about my will and my will is that if my daughter Sarah Keley should dy before her husband John Keley : that yet my housall goods both beding brasse & puter with the other things in the house after John Kelys death may remaine vnto my daughter Saras Children as ther father John Keley while he lives do see have most need of it : I say the Children of his body.

Likwise I do desir my two Loving ffrends m^r Nicholas Noie and Robert Long to be my ouer seers that my will may be performed and according to the time. p me RICHARD KNIGHT.

Signed Seled and apointed
to be in ffore after my deceas   Seal
(This to lines that is struk out in
the 11 and twelv lines was Struk out
before the Signig and Seling was don
Witnes   Nicholas Noyes
                 Robert Long
Proved 25 September 1683.

RICHARD LOWLE.

Bee it knowne vnto all men by these p^{r}sents that I Richard Lowle of Newbury in the Countie of Essex Newe: Massac: being sencible of mine owne weaknes & mortality being of perfect memorie doe here make my last will & Testament coffiending my soule into the hands of my blessed Sauiour & Redeemer the Lord Jesus Christ: and my body to the earth from whence it was taken, In assured hope of a happy Resurrection in the day of the appearing of Jesus christ. And for my worldly Goods I dispose of as followeth.

Imp^r: I giue and bequeath vnto my loucing & beloued wife Margeret, all my houshold Goods (except my great Bible, and my great pot) & Chattells, with house & land & orchard and meadow, dureing her widdowhood, or naturall life if shee remaine a widdow. also I appoint my said wife to bee my sole executrix of this my last will & testament And after her I giue & bequeath vnto my son Perciuall Lowle, all my house & Barne & outhouseing & orchard with all my land adioyneing to my house (except twelue acres on the northeasterly side of my Land) also I giue to my Son Perciuall my twelue acres of Marsh in the great marshes by the Pumb bushes, and fiue acres of marsh or meadow below Beniamin Rolfes, and two acres of my marsh of the eight acres at old Towne, and also the one halfe of my freehold & preuiledg of Coffimonnag and my great pot & my great Bible. And I do hereby acknowledg that the meadow in Birchen meadows which was formerly mine to bee my Son Percinalls by purchase

Also I giue and bequeath to my Son Thomas Lowle twelue acres of my vpland adioyneing to James Brownes and Nathaniel Clarks land & widdow Muzzyes land, So much in breadth at the street as ruffing the whole length, bearing an equall breadth as shall amount to twelue acres. Alwayes prouided that if my son Samuell Lowle desire one acre of land to build an house for his setled habitation, then my son Thomas shall let my son Samuell haue an acre adioyneing to the widdow Muzzyes land foure Rods in front next the street and forty Rods in length, but if my Son Samuell shall refuse or relinquish his Right in the acre of land, as in this my will abousaid by mee giuen. Then my son Thomas shall pay to my said Son Samuell six pound in currant Newengl: siluer mony or ten pound in Currant pay. Also I giue to my Sonne Thomas Lowle all my Plumb Iland Lott of Marsh Land, and six acres of my eight acres of salt Marsh at the old Towne marsh, also I giue to him the other halfe of my freehold or preuiledg in Comoning or Comon lands. And after my wiues decease, I giue all my houshold goods, & moucables: of what kind soeuer within or without doores, to be equally diuided between my two sons Perciuall Lowle & Thomas Lowle or their heires, also I giue all my liueing stock of Cattell to my Son Tho: Lowle Also I giue liberty to my Sonne Thomas Lowle to liue in the house & to haue the sixt part of the Apples yearly so long as he liues a single man without a wife and no longer, and I giue a booke called m^r Hookers politic vnto Anthony Somerby, my debts & funerall being discharged by my executrix, I do hereby declare this to be my last will & Testament Renownceing & makeing Null all former wills by mee made & herevnto I set my hand & seale June 25th 1681

signed & sealed in psence of   RICHARD LOWLE   Seal
     Tristram Coffin
     Anthony Somerby.
Proved 26 September 1682.

HENRY ROLFE.

The 15th 12th month 1642

I desire to comend my soule into the hands of the Lord Jesus Christ, I desire my goods may be equally divided to my wife & all my children, only my sonne John Roffe must have the house & lands more then all the rest of my children and that their porcoñs shalbe divided when they be 21 yeares of age if they marry not before In case my wife dye or marry then the goods shalbe divided; otherwise not till my eldest childe come to be 21 yeares of age But still to remayne in their mothers hands with the rest till that either of them are 21 yeares of age or marry If any of my children dye then that porcoñ shalbe equally divided betweene my wife & the rest of my children I doe give vnto my wife one great brasse pott and one great brasse pann and a great brasse posnett and a chafingdish and five pewter platters I doe give vnto my Kinsman Thomas Whittear a swarme of bees. I desire my brother John Roffe and my Cosen John Saunders of Sallisbery and William Moudy of Newberry to oversee my will & order it to my desire & accordinge to my will
Witnes herevnto I set my hand

     Thomas Hale   HENRY ROFFE.
     Thomas Cowllman
     William Mose
This will was proved in Ipswich Court 28th first mo: 1643.

HONOUR ROLFE.

Henry Largin of Charlstowne*   house of Thomas
Blanchard on n   where widdow Honour Rolfe lay
berry lay sick, shee did declare h
be; that her sonne Beniamin Rolfe should haue the substance of her estate, which was her owne & pp estate, & that
he should be her sole Executor. Only she gaue these pticulers
as followeth, her bedding & clothes linnen and woollen she gaue to
be equally deuided betwixt her two daughters. Also shee gaue
twenty shillings a piece to her foure grand children to be giuen them
five yeares after her death. Also one little Cowe she gaue to her
Daughter yt lines at Newberry. Also of foure peeces of Brasse shee
gaue two to her sonne Beniamin, which he should Choose, & to each
of her daughters one. The rest she gaue to her sonne Beniamine,
saucing two pewter platters which she gaue to each of her daughters
one, & further shee exprest her mind about a Barne that is built vpon
pt of her sonne Beniamins ground, she gaue to her sonne John Rolfe
all her interest in the ground that the Barne stood vpon. this is the
substance of her expression as farr as he can remember

memorandum that pt of the 22 the whole 23. 24 & pt of yᵉ 25 lines
were blotted out

RI. BELLINGHAM

Taken vpon oath by the said Henry Largin this 20-12-1650.
who further saith that the said Honor Rolfe was of a disposeing
memory before me Ri. Bellingham.

The Testymoney of George Vaghan Aged abought 23 yeares Concerning the last will of Honoʳ Rolfe widdow deceased: 19th of 10th
mᵒ 1650.

This Deponent saith that himselfe being in prsence together with
Henry Largin some two daies before the death of the aboue said
testator, he heard her make this her last will in maner following.

Inprimis She bequeathed all her estate in generall to her yongest
Sonne Beniamine Rolfe onely excepted these pticulers which follow:

Item to her foure Grand Children she gaue twenty shillings apece,
to be paid them foure or fiue yeare after that time, Item all her Right
in halfe an acre of Ground on which the Barne stands and a youge
sowe she gaue to her sonne John Rolfe:

Item a little Cowe that she had she gaue to her daughter Hanah
Dole.

Item all her wearcing Cloathes & bedding she gaue to be equally
deuided betweene her two Daughters Anna and Hanah: these
pticulers aboue said this deponent tooke spetiall notice of; & further
he saith not: only a day after her sonne in lawe Richard Dole comeing
to her desired this Deponent to Aske her what she would doe with

---

the three pounds ten shillings in England, & shee Answered that she would that her sonne Beniamine should haue a sute of Cloathes out of it, & the rest he should haue meaning her said sonne in Lawe Richard Dole.

The word Beniamine enterlined.

Taken upon oath this 20th of the 12th m° 1650 before me William Hibbins.

The Court vpon the Testimonyes of George Vaughan & Henry Largin of Charles towne as fare as there Testimonys doe agree is the will & Testam.t of Honour Rofe & by them pued in the Court held at Ipswich the 30th of (7) 1651.

By me Robert Lord Cleric.

Mrs KATHERINE COYTMORE.

The last will & testament of Katherin Coytemoore widdow dwelling in Charlestowne in New England, written ye thirtieth day of ye second moneth one thousand sixe hundred fifty & eight.

I Katherin Coytmoore of Charlestowne aforesaid doe heerby make this my last will & testam.t in manner & forme as followes; being at p.rsent in health of body & minde.

Inp: I comend my soule to God, & my body I comend to my children & friends to be decently buried.

It: I give & bequeath vnto ye fower children of my sonne Will Ting of Boston, (formerly deceased) vid. Elizab; Anna, Bethia & Mercy Ting Two hundred pounds, wch said two hundred pounds I formerly delivered into their father Will Tings hands, as will appeare by a bond vnder his hand in my custody.

It: I give & bequeath vnto these fower vid Elizab; Anna, Bethia & Mercy Ting a house & an orchard & other ground by it scituat & being in ye Neecke of land at Charlestowne and adioyning to ye Ferry wch passeth over to Maulden, likewise tenn acres of land more or lesse lying at Menatomyes, & a parcell of medow lying at Wormewoods poynt; all wch house & land aforesaid were once ye possession of Mr Abr: Palmer.

It: I give & bequeath vnto ye said Elizab, Anna, Bethia & Mercy Ting my eight part of ye mill wch Jn° Fownell houlds in Charlestowne, as alsoe three Cow Comons.

It: I give & bequeath vnto Elizab. Ting two Persia Carpetts & a boxe of East India dishes, & two fayre window Cushins.

It: I give & bequeath vnto Anna Ting my red sattin Quilt, my Turky Carpett, & my great lookeing glasse, a screetore, & a boxe of trenchers.

It: I give & bequeath vnto Bethia Ting my needleworke cloth Carpett, and a boxe of East India dishes, & ye Court Cubbert cloth belonging therunto.

2

It: I give & bequeath vnto Mercy Ting my Pantadoe Quilt, as alsoe a payre of my best Curtaynes & vallants.

It: I giue & bequeath to yᵉ fiue children of my sonne Increase Nowell, vid: Samuel, Mehetabell, Increase, Mary, & Alexander; & to yᵉ fiue children of my daughter Katherin Graves, vid Thomas, Nathaniel, Joseph, Rebecka & Susana Graves, one dwelling house lately inhabited by my selfe, now inhabited by Mʳ Tho: Shepheard neer to yᵉ meeting house in Charlestowne; concerning wᶜʰ house & ground therto belonging it is my will yᵗ it shall be sould by my Executrixes, & yᵉ produce therof to be equally devided by my Executrixes to yᵉ fiue children of my sonne Increase Nowell, & yᵉ fiue children of my daughter Katherin Graves above mentioned.

It: I give & bequeath to my grandchilde Sarah Williams,* all my land wᶜʰ yᵉ Towne of Charlestowne hath given me lying & being at Woborne, & at Misticke side, as alsoe fower pounds in household goods.

It: I give & bequeath vnto yᵉ Pastoʳ of yᵉ Ch: of Charlestowne Mʳ Zach: Symes yᵉ sũme of fiue pounds.

It: I give & bequeath to Margarett Hutchison twenty shillings.

It: I giue & bequeath to Widow Nash twenty shills.

It: I giue & bequeath to Ann yᵉ wife of Tho: Carter twenty shills.

It: I giue & bequeath to Deacon Rob: Hale all such portions of land as were given out to me on Maulden side in yᵉ yeare one thousand sixe hundred fifty & eight, together wᵗʰ forty shills & desyre yᵗ he would performe yᵉ office of overseer to this my will.

It: I give & bequeath vnto Elizab, Anna, Bethia & Mercy the Children of Will Ting   [Blank in the original.]

It: my will is yᵗ all yᵉ legacies before mentioned, shall be reserved & kept in my Executrixes hands a full halfe yeare after my decease, & then to be payd by them.

But if any person or persons to whome I have bequeathed any thinge as before mentioned, be not contented wᵗʰ my last will & yᵉ perticulers therein bequeathed, but shall causelessly molest, trouble, vex or cause to be troubled either of my two Executrixes, or any of their heyres, Executors, administrators, or Assignes, then I doe recall from any such soe doeing, my former guift or gifts, & I only bequeath vnto him or her soe molesting as abovesaid fiue shills out of my whole estate & noe more.

And I doe appoynt & ordayne my two daughters Parnell Nowell & Katherin Graves to be my sole Executrices of this my last will & Testamᵗ to both wᶜʰ I doe bequeath yᵉ rest of my vnbequeathed goods.

It: To Martha Cogin widow of Mʳ Jnᵒ Cogin I give one silver wine Cup.

                              CATHREN COITMORE
                                   Seal.

* This was probably the daughter of Parnel Nowell by her first husband Parker.

Signed, sealed & witnessed in yᵉ presence of vs whose names arc hecrvnto
subscribed this 30ᵗʰ day of yᵉ second
moneth in yᵉ yeare of oʳ Lord one
thousand sixe hundred fifty & eight.

Thomas Starr
Robert Hale
John Wightman.

Proved 27 December 1659.

TRISTRAM COFFIN.

In the name of God amen I Tristram Coffin of Newbury In the
Countey of Essex Masachusett provans New england I being sensa-
bell of my owne martallity and at this time of a desposing mind dow
mak this as my last Will and testament comiting my Sole to God In
and tharow the marrits of Jesus Christ and my boody to the dust in
hops of a joyfull Resuarection and as for my wourldly goods which
God hath geuen me I despose of them as follocth

1.   I dou hear by ordar and appoyent my son Nathanuel Coffin to
take spesshall care of my wife his mothar to prouid for har in all
Respectes duoring har life all things nessesary for har comfortabell
being both In sicknis and in heleth.

2.   My Will is and I dou hear by geue to my son James Coffin to
him his heirs and assigns the hous he now leuith in and the shop the
two barns next his hous and on half of the pastuor land ajoyning
Including his orchard as part of it that side next maiar March is land,
soo much frunt as from March is land to half way the Cow yeard
betwen the Barns : as allso all the plowland I bouft of John Long and
Shuball : to In Ioy the 3 acres and a half with in one year aftar my
death and tou partes of ficue of all coman priviligis.   In the twons
comans : and the one half part of my orchard and pastuor land at
Trotters bridg : and one half of the meddow I bouft of Parsifill Lowle :
and fower acres of that meddow a joyning to deacon Colin Noys all
the leneght of the medow of equall bredth at both ends : and seuen
acres of meddo at Jeryco which I bouft of Mr Dole and a lot of
meddo at Plumb Iland which I bouft of Richard Jackman. and the
othar pece of meddow which I bouft of Jackman, at ould twon : and
and the seven acres of meddow at Salesbury beach : and two partes
of ficue of my free hold lots : and one half of the woudland I bouft
of Edmon Moores and one theird part of the Rate lot I bouft of
Joseph Plumer and one halfe of the Rate lot at John Emoris Meddow : Including that .6. acres which the Comety grantid him to be
part of it and one halfe of the woud lot lately laid out which joynith
to Richard Browns lot. and docktar Topans : and all that lot of upland which lieth in Salesbury. which I bouft of Mr Bayley all wais
prouidid that my son James Coffin pay to his brothar Nathanuell

Coffin fortey shillins a year duaring his mothars life to be paid In or as money far har supply.

3   My will is and I dow geue to my son Stephen Coffin to him his heirs and assigns all my housing and upland and meddows with priviligis of Comman Reights belonging to me in hauerhill. and all my meddo within the bounds of Mr Hookes farme. and all my meddow at Plumb Iland at the North end of the Iland callid the hundrid acres: and one fifte part of Comman Reights in Newbury: and one fift part of my free hould lotes. and one theird part of the Rate lot I bouft of Joseph Plumer. he paiing to his son Tristram fieue pounds

4   My will is I geue to my son Petar Coffin to him his heirs and assigns for euer the farm at glostar with the Iland and all priuiligis in Coman within the tuon ship of glostar the which I have geuen him a deed of: and I geve him six shillins and I dou hear by ordar my said son Petar Coffin: to pay to his brothar Nathanuell Coffin all that Is due to me from him ethar by book bill. or bond: and the 6^lb a year that my wife should rescue of him annally. duoring har natural life becas my son Nathanuell must provid for his mothar.

5:   My will Is and I dou geue to my son Nathanuel Coffin to him. his heirs and assigns my now dwelling hous with my barnes and pastuor land a joyning and archards so much frunt as from Richard Browns land to half way the cow yeard: betwen the barns: and two partes of fieue of all Coman Reights in Newbury and all my Plowland a joyning to Joseph Downers land: and the one half of my archard and pastuar land at Trotters bridg and one half of the wood land I bouft of Edmon Moore: and the one halfe of my Rate lot at Emaris meddow: Including my son Jamses is .6. acres as part of it: and the one theird part of the Rate lot I bouft of Joseph Plumer. and 2 parts of fieue of my free howld lots: and that Rat lot that I bouft of Hugh March and Hains. by John Browns uper hous ajoyning to the land Petar Coffin bouft of John Bartlet and all my medow at littell Pin Iland. and all the .6. acres I bouft of Nath Badger. and all the medow. bouft of the longs fl of Danil Osolloway: cesepting the .4. acres geuen to James: and half the medow I bouft of Parsifell Lowle: and all the medow at JeRecow one the north east sid of the creek. and fower lots at Plumb Iland of meddo: Whelars lot and Smith .2. lots and Grenlef lot: and the one halfe of the woud lot lately laid out liing betwen Richard Browns and dockter Toppans: as allso all my howhowld goods and cattell and shep: and swine and harsis and all othar things belonging to me and all my debtes due to me by book bills ad bonds or othar wise.

6.   My will is I geue to my grand son Tristram Sambron: fower pounds to be paid to him by his fathar out of the money I lent him to by meddow with. and the Remaindar I geue to my daftar Judeth.

7   Itam I geue to my daftar Deborah Knight 5^s and: twelf walnot trese: In that land I bouft of Edman Moores: ad to har son Tristram Knight a cowe.

8 I geue to my daftar Marey Littel 5ˢ ad to har son Tristram Littel a cow and .2. Shep:

9: I geue to my daftar Lidea Pike: 5ˢ:

10. I geue to my grand daftar Marey Littell a fethar bed and bostar and pillo. and apar of blinkits and 2 couer leds and 2 pare of shetes.

11. my will is and I dou hear by appoyent my son Nathanuell Coffin to be the exccutar of this my will to pay all my honist deptes and to rescue all my debtes. and to par forme the legissis according to this my will and to take speshall care of his mothar In har age and I dou Renouns all formar wils by me made ad declar this to be my last will as witnis my hand and sail this .12. dy of May 1703 ad in the Second year of the Reign of our Souerin lady Quen Ann of england ec.

Signid Selid ad ownid in the presens of

Richʳᵈ Brown junʳ   TRISTRAM COFFIN
Anthony Somerby
Nicolas Pettingell   Seal

Proved 23 February 1704.

STEPHEN GREENLEAF.

Because I know not ye day of my death I make this my last will & testament I bequeath my bodye to yᵉ Earth & my Soule to god yᵗ gave itt In hope of a blessed Resurrection.

1. I Give to my eldest sone Stephen Greenleif yᵉ one halfe of my house Lott that half next him, he making all yᵉ ffence that lyeth against his owne land, I give him also my share of yᵉ Island that wee bought betwixt vs of Ephraim Winslowe of salisbury with two acres of yᵉ meadow below yᵉ Island next Caleb Moodyes Meadow Provided yᵗ. there bee liberty for Edmund to make a ffence a Crosse yᵉ Island from my ditche to Doctʳ Dole his Ditche, And wᵗᵗ wood may bee upon yᵉ Island may bee vsed to repaire yᵉ ffence, And yᵗ my sone Stephen wᵗʰ his brother Edmund & Caleb Moody yᵗ is Engaged do yʳ proportion of yᵉ ffence to secure their meadow.

2ⁿᵈˡʸ I give to my sone John Greenleif besides wᵗᵗ he hath already had my ffreehold lott, att plum Island, he paying to his sister Mary five pounds in paye when she shall bee married or att Eighteen years of age.

3ᵈˡʸ I give to my sone Samˡˡ Greenleif besides yᵉ living he hath by deed of gift, five sheepe & all my waring Clothes.

4ᵗʰˡʸ I give my sone Tristram that living att Hartychoake yᵉ ffreehold lott wᵗʰ the housing & ffences to itt, & yᵉ two River Lotts of Saltmarsh att fox Island, He paying to his sister Mary five pounds in pay, when she shall be married or att eighteen years of Age.

5ᵗʰˡʸ I give my Rate Lott to be equaly divided between Jnᵒ Samˡˡ

Tristram & Edmund as equally as they can, they drawing Lotts for y^r shares, And ye Rate Lott I bought of Benj^a Gutridge, I give to my soñe Stephen, I doe Apoint also my soñe Stephen to pay unto his sister Mary three score pounds in pay & ten pounds in money within two years after she shall bee eighteen years of age or Marriage.

6^{thly} I giue to my soñe Stephen ye Chafer, To Daughter Dole ye brass pot or ye litle Iron Kettle w^e she will, And ye little silver Cup in my Cupboard and one Sheep; And I doe hereby owne that I gave him ye meadow att Salisbury next Major Pikes pasture, that he should have had a deed of gift of. I give to my daught^r Noyce my great platter, & ye silver wine Cup to her daughter Elizabeth, I give ye Coaker Nutt Cup to my soñe Stephen.

7^{thly} I give to my soñe Edmund Greenleif ye Rest of my estate, Housing, Land, & meadow, fence, stocke & houshold stuff & tooles, he paying to his sister Mary Swett Eight pounds in pay, assoone as she shall be married.

Lastly. In Case my soñe Edmund Greenleif should dye wth out Issue Lawfully begotten of his owne bodye Then all wch I have in this my will given to him I give unto my soñe Stephen Greenleife viz: Houses Lands &c as before mentioned, He paying to ye Rest of his brothers & sisters y^n surviving proportionable ye vallew w^{tt} itt may bee valued att, by two indifferent men, Reserving to himself & Mary wch I freely give three parts or shares of ye s^d Edmunds Portion;

I Appoint my soñe Edmund Greenleife to be my Sole Executo^r & Caleb Moody & Wm Titcombe to see this my will performed as overseers of ye same. My desire is y^t my well beloved wife shall live wth my soñe Edmund, butt if in Case my wife should see good to Remove & live other where, then Edmund shall pay to his Mother foure pounds a yeare or else she to have ye thirds of ye Land; And further in Case my soñe Tristram dye wthout Issue Lawfully begotten of his owne body, then ye one half of ye Vallew of ye land given him by mee, to bee to his widdowe & ye other half to be divided Equaly amongst ye Rest of ye children In full testimony that this is my Last Will & testament I haue hereunto putt my hand & Seale this 5th day of august 1690.

STEPHEN GRENLEFE   Seal

Wittnesse hereunto

This was published to bee ye last Will & testament of Capt Stephen Greenleif sen^r & signed & sealed in p^{r}sence of

     Benj^a Gerrish   in p^{r}sence of us
     Willm Longfellow
     James March.

Proved 25 November 1690.

HENRY JAQUES.

In the name of God and by his Assistance I Henry Jaques of Newbury do humbly cõmit my soule body & spirit both in life and death into the everlasting arms of God All sufficient my Heavenly ffather and to Jesus Christ my alone Saviour & Blessed Redeemer through yᵉ Power & Presents of his Eternall Spirit my body to yᵉ earth whence its origenall was taken in hope of an Happy & Glorious Resurrection in yᵉ Great day of the man Christ Jesus to whome be Glory forever. Amen.

And for such Good things of this world as it hath pleased God in this my Pilgrimage to cõmitt to my Stuardship I (as much as in me is) dispose as is heerafter expressed—

Impˢ. I Give to An my dear & loving wife the one half of my dwelling house & one half of the Great Celler & one third part of my orchyard wᵗʰ ten Rods of sutable ground for a Garden to be kept sufficiently fenced as also fire wood sufficient for her use to be ready cutt and brought to the dore for her as also two cows out of my stock at her choice to be wintered and sũmered for her, together wᵗʰ the bed in the parlor with all the ffurniture belonging to the same all which she shall be seised of imediatly after my decease & to be performed by my execut' heerafter named together wᵗʰ a liberty of keeping two swine as also she shall have a horse & man provided by my sᵈ executor to carry her to Meeting or otherwise as she shall have occasion all which my sᵈ wife shall injoy during her widdowhood, as also six pounds pʳ Añum to be yearly paid by my execut' during her naturall life ; As also one half of all my houshold goods to be for her use during her naturall life & then to be disposed of by her amõng her children as she shall se cause. But if she shall se cause to live wᵗʰ my execut' he providing all things necessary for her then that shall be in leiv of yᵉ payments afore mentioned all, wᶜʰ is in leiv of her thirds.

Item. To my son Daniell Jaquis I Give all that my Land in Bradford & Rowley that 1 formerly bought of Capᵗ Walker of Bradford, both upland & meadow together wᵗʰ all the priveledges & appurtenances thereunto be belonging, as also all my house & land in Almsbury wᶜʰ I Bought of Richard Currier & John Gimpson wᵗʰ all yᵉ priviledges belonging thereunto Also all my Right in the Saw mill there wᵗʰ all yᵉ priviledges therof. Also that sixty Acres of land be it more or less wᶜʰ I bought of Robert Jones of Almsbury & lying in Almsbury wᵗʰ all yᵉ priviledges therof also all that peice of salt marish in plumb Iland lying in the Hundred acres, being five or six Acres be it more or less, Also one of my divisions in yᵉ six thousand Acres in the upper cõmons in Newbury either that wᶜʰ shall fall to me by my ffreehold or that wᶜʰ will fall to me by Mʳ Richardsons Rate of Ano 1685 which he shall choose, but if the said cõmons be not divided by the rule that is now proposed, then he shall have the one half of what shall fall to me by my freehold or otherwise in any other division that shall be made in time to come in the s^d Six thousand Acres all wch I give to him my son Daniell Jaquis and to his heyrs & Assignes forever.

Item. To my Daughter Mary the wife of Richard Browne I Give twenty pounds to be paid by my executor out of my stock within one year after my decease; Besids what I formerly gave her.

Item. To my Daughter Hañah the wife of Ephraim Plumer having formerly given her, her portion I do now give her forty Shillings more to be paid by my Executor.

Item. To my Daughter Sarah the wife of John Hale I give five-teene povnds besids what I have formerly Given her to be paid by my executor.

Item. To my daughter Elisabeth I give fifty povnds to be paid by my executor within two years after her Mariage or when she shall attaine unto the age of twenty one years but if she should dye before the said portion is payable leaving no child that then the said portion shall be equally divided among her surviuing brothers & sisters.

Item. To my Daughter Ruth I give ffifty Pounds to be paid by my executor wth in two years aftar her Marriage or when she shall attaine unto the Age of Twenty one years but if she should dye before her said Portion is dew leaving no child that than her s^d Portion shall be equally apportioned among her surviving Brothers & sisters.

Item. To my daughter Abigaell I give fifty pounds to be paid by my executor within two years after her Mariage or when she shall attaine unto the age of Twenty years but if she should dye before her s^d Portion be dew that then it shall be equally divided among her surviuing brothers & sisters Provided she leave no child

Item. My Will is that for my Grand-son Henry the son of my Son Henry Jaquis (deceased) that he shall at the charge of my executor be maintained & kept at schoole untill he can read and write well and cast account sufficiently for coñon uses & then to be bound Apprentice to Som Trade And when he shall attaine vnto the age of twenty one years he shall be paid by my executor the sum of fiveteen pounds but if my s^d Grand-son shall dye before ye s^d Legacy be payable then it shall be equally divided among my surviving children.

Item. And ffor my estate Lying in Woodbridg Towne in the Province of East-Newjersy my will is that it shall be divided Among the three sons of my Son Henry Jaquis Late of Woodbridg towne (deceased) to his Eldest son a duble share.

Item. To my Grand-son Richard ye son of my son Richard Jaquis (deceased) I give the sum of fifty povnds to be paid by my executor when he shall attaine unto the age of twenty one years but if he ye s^d Richard should dye before ye s^d Legacy be payable that then ye s^d legasy shall be equally divided among my surviving children.

Farther. I do heerby make and appoint my Son Stephen Jaquis to be my trve and lawfull Heyre and do accordingly give & bequeth unto him all my housing & Lands & ffrechold wth all my Goods & chattells together wth all those debts that now are or heerafter may appeere to be dew unto me by bill Bond or otherwise together with all those libertyes & priviledges that I have or heerafter may appeer to be my right (excepting alwayes such gifts & Legacies which are in this my last will & Testament contained) all other my housing & land both upland & meadow I do give to him my s^{d} Son Stephen Jaquis as is above expressed to him & his heyres forever But if my s^{d} Son Stephen shall dye leaving no Heyr of his body Lawfully begotten that then my said housing & lands shall be and remaine to my son Daniell Jaquis to him & his heyrs forever. And if my son Daniell should dye leaving no Heyr Male of his body Lawfully begotten then my said housing and lands shall be and remaine to my Grand-Son Richard Jaquis aforenamed to him & his heyrs forever and if he should dye Leaving no heyre of his body lawfully begotten, then my sd housing & Lands to be & Remaine unto ye Heyre Male of my family fforever.

Item. My Will is that wheras Jasper my Indian hath been a good Servant to me my will is that he shall serve my executor well & faithfully Six years after my decease & y^{t} then he shall have his freedom being by my executor set at liberty & I do heerby will & appoint him to do it.

Farther I do Appoint my son Stephen Jaquis to be the executor of this my last Will & Testament my Lawfull debts & funerall charges to be by him paid & discharged.

Lastly I do desire & appoint my christian freinds Capt Thomas Noyes & Mr Moses Gerrish to be overseers of the dew performance of this my last will & Testament heerby Willing & requiring my executor to satisfy for what time & paines they shall spend therin.

In Wittness of all & singuler ye premesis as my last Will & Testament I have heerunto set my hand & Seale this thirtieth of october one thousand six hundred eighty & six

memorandum before the sealing & wittnessing hereof I declare my will is y^{t} wheras I have given my wife in this my last will six pounds p^{r} Añum during her naturall life my will is that it should be paid to her by my executer in three bush: of wheat & ye rest of it one half in english graine & ye other half in Indian corne.

HENRY JAQUES Seal

Signed Sealed and declared
in ye presens of us
    Isack Ilsley
    Anthony Mors
    Henry Short.
Proved 8 March 1687.

In the name of God & by his Assistance I Richard Dole sen^r of Newbury in the County of Essex in the province of the Massachusetts Bay in New England Do Humbly comitt my Soule Body and Spirit both in life and Death into the everlasting Arms of God all sufficient my Heavenly ffather and unto Jesus christ my alone Saviour and Blessed Redeemer thru' the Power and presents of his eternall Spirit, my Body to the Earth whence its origenall was Taken, in Hope of a Happy and Glorious Resurection in Great Day of the man Christ Jesus to him be Glory both now & ever Amen.

And for such Good things of this world as God hath been pleased in this my Pilgrimage to Comitt to my Stuardship, I as much as in me is do dispose as is heerafter expressed.

Imp I Give to Patience my Deare & loving wife (besides what I Promised her uppon our Mariage by a writing under my hand & seale bearing Date Octob^r 29th 1690 acknowledged by me before the Worshipf^{ll} Nathani^{ll} Saltingstall Esqr) I Do now give her the use of the Bed & Bedding together wth all other the furniture that I shall leave in my Parlour during the time that she remaines my Widow, As also eight cord of wood p^r Añum to be brought & laid convenient to the house by the charg of my execut^{rs} heerafter named during the Time afore sd, Also I give her my now Riding Horse, and my Bridle, sadle and Pilion, and also two Cows at her owne choyce & also two shoates which I giue to my said wife ffreely foreuer, the said Cows & horse to be wintered and summered by the charg of my execut^{rs} during my wives remaining my widow but if the Horse or Cows should faile thru age from being servisable my wife shall be supplyed by my Execut^{rs} wth such which shall be good & servisable at my execut^{rs} charge, Also I give my sd wife two Rods square of Ground neer my now dwelling house for a Garden where shee shall choose to be fenced well and so to be maintained at the charg of my execut^{rs}, and so to remaine unto her during her being my Widow, ffarther I giue to my said wife six Bushills of good winter Apples yearly and a Hogshead to Putt them into, and one Barrell of Sider yearly, also I give her the use of all the Glasses and Galle-potts in my cubbord, Also a good peice of land sufficient to sow half a Peck of flax-seed yearly out of my owne land at her owne choyce all which shee shall enjoy during her being my widow, Also I give to her my said wife ffreely for Euer twenty pounds of Good cotten wooll & twenty pounds of Good fllax teer & thirty pounds of Good sheeps wooll, Also the linen wheele that she useth to spin on, also one good Cotten wheele & a peir of good Cards, also one p^r of sheets & one Blanket also a fyre pan & warming Pan, Also twenty Bushills of Good indian Corne, and four Bushills of Rye and two Bushills of wheat & half a Barrell of my Pork & half a Barrell of Beife and twenty shillings in Mony, and four Bushills of Malt and a good Sack,

also my Trunk also two Ews and two Lambs, all which to be delivered to her by my executors Imediatly after my Death together
with one fifth part of all my household goods, Also I give to my said
wife the use of my Still during her widdowhood as also the use of
that Roome usualy called the shopp during her remaining my widow
shee being at the charg to make away into the same.

Ite   To the Heyrs of my son John Dole late of Newbury deceased
besides what I have formerly Given him by Deed of gift, I Do now
give him al the rest of the Housing & lands, wharffs and ware house
wher they now dwell belonging to me that were not mentioned in
said Deed of Gift, together wth the other half of the pasture neer
Peter Godfrys land wth the other half of the meadow at Salisbury
bought by me of Mr Sanders: and the other half of Rings Iland
the one half of which parcells of land housing & wharfs I formerly
gave him as in my Deed to him more at larg may appeer, also I give
to them Sixteen acres of land lying uppon an Iland against Haverhill in Merrimack River be it more or less Purchased of Robert
Clement & others also five comonages in Haverhill Purchased of
Joseph Davis, also my Rights in the Playnes of Haverhill Purchased
of Robert Clement, Also my Great Bible, Also my ffouling Peice and
musquet that are now in theyr hands, also my negro Boy named Tom,
and this shall be the Ballance of all accounts that ever hath been
between my said son John Dole & myself Farther my will is that
my Daughter in law the widow of my said son John Dole viz m^{rs}
Mary Dole shall haue the possession & improvement of all the aboue
mentioned Housing and lands & the rest During her remaining my
said sons widow.

Ite.   To my son Richard Dole besides what I have formerly given
him by Deed of Gift I giue him eight acres of meadow or marsh be
it more or less which was formerly Granted by the Towne of Newbury to Henry Rolfe and by me purchassed of John Rolfe which said
Marsh Joyneth to the ends of the four acre lotts and is Bounded
westerly By a great creeke   Also I give him one eighth part of my
upland & meadow or marsh on plumb Iland lying in Newbury &
Rowley Bounds, he renouncing that parcell of upland & meadow in
plumb Iland mentioned in his Deed of gift, ffarther I give him Pastur-
ring for three cows and one horse in my pasture as now it is to him
& his heyrs for ever   He and his bearing a proportionable share in
fencing and Trenching the said Pasture as there shall be need, Also
I give to him what is Due from him to me uppon my Booke being
about sixty or seaventy pounds.   Also I giue him one half of my Bark
house & mill and of all my other Implements of Tañing, Also one
half of my Tan house and Tan-yard and Pitts wth eighty Rods of
land, on the northerly side of the works to be laid out from the
Green to the Gutter so as may be most convenient for a Tañing
designe   The one half of the said land that the Bark house pitts and
Tan house stands on to be part of the eighty Rods, with this Pro-

viso that neither he nor his shall haue liberty to sett up a dwelling house on the said eighty Rods or any part therof nor shall any person Dwell thereuppon, But it shall be in his Liberty to haue his diuision made & the eighty Rod to be laid out when he or his heyrs pleses alwayes Reserving that peice of land knowne by the name of the Grass platt to my Son William Dole & his heyrs for ever & for my wife during her widowhood to make use of. Also I giue to my said son Richard Dole one half of the hides and leather that belongs to me in the Pitts or else where, Also I giue him one third part of my woodland in Dea⁰ Noys his neck all this I giue to my said son to him & his heyrs fforever wᵗʰ this Proviso that neither he nor his heyrs demand nothing of me nor my execut⁽ˢ⁾ for any work or Labour done by him formerly about Tañing, also I giue to him my said son one fifth part of all my houshold Goods, also one quarter of my hay Boate also one third part of my vtinsills of Husbandry & of my Tooles.

Ite. I Giue to my son William Dole & his heyrs forever my Dwelling house that I now dwell in together wᵗʰ my Barnes & other my out housing wᵗʰ the lands that they now stand on wᵗʰ the land next adjacent both upland & meadow to the heads of the Lotts wᵗʰ my orchards theron & so to the River and the other end or side is Bounded by an easterly line from Blumfeilds old house to the Heads of the Lotts, by a west line to the Greene together with fiue Lotts four acres a Peice be they more or less viz Spencers Lott, ffrancklings Lott, Nathaniʰ Badgers Lott & two Lotts knowne by the name of Moodeys Lotts together wᵗʰ all the Rye field & land adjoyning together wᵗʰ the Salt Marsh called the pasture excepting only the eighteen acres at the lower end next to Eastons creek, Also I giue him all the lands lying between the Lotts & the Riuer Also I giue him one third part of the Ilands of fllatt belonging to me in the Great Riuer, Also one quarter part of my upland and marsh in plumb Iland lying pᵗˡʸ in Newbury and pᵗˡʸ in Rowley Bounds, Also my Rate Lott lying on Bradford line, Also one half of my Marsh knowne by the name of Jerecho Marsh Also my negro Boy named Mingo, Also I giue him all the diuision or diuisions of land that shall be laid out in the coῆons of Newbury to Mʳ Edmund Greenlefs freehold which was by me formerly purchassed, Also I giue him one third pt of all my Implements & utinsills of Husbandry & Tooles, also I giue him one third part of my wood land next Henry Shorts pasture, and one third part of my ten acres of woodland in Deaꞔ noyes his neck also one half of my Haye Boate, also one quarter part of the hides & leather that Do belong to me in the Pitts or elce whear also one fether Bedd, also one fifth part of all my household Goods all which I Do giue to my son william Dole, excepting what is before mentioned in this my last Will & Testament and otherwise disposed of ffarther I giue to him my said son one half of that peice of Marsh knowne by the name of the ffour acres all which I giue to

my said son William Dole (Reserving eight Rods of Ground out of
the land to him mentioned, for my son Abner Dole as is heerafter
giuen him)

5½ lines cancelled as recorded post

Iĩ. To my son Abner Dole I giue the new house in which he now
dwells together wth three four acre Lotts therunto adjoyning viz
Randols Lott and two Lotts which I Bought of Lieu^t Pike Also
twelue acres of Salt Marsh adjoyning to the six acres which I gaue
my son Richard Dole which is at the Lower end of the Pasture next
Estons creek Also the third part of the Ilands of fflatts belonging to
me in the Great River Also the half of my Marsh in Quantity &
Quality called Jericho Marsh Also the fourth part of upland & marsh
which I haue in Plumb Iland partly in Newbury & partly in Rowley
Bounds, Alwayes reserving at the upper ends of the Lotts aboue
given a way of three Rods broad for his Brother William & his heyrs
to pass and repass to and from his lands, Also I giue my said son
one third part of my woodland next unto Henry Shorts pasture,
Also my ffreehold purchase of Thomas Blumfield wth the priviledges
therunto belonging or that may arise therby also one third part of
my woodland lying in Dea͠ Noyes his Neck, Also three acres & a
half of land co͠monly called Shorts Lott, Also one fifth part of all
my household Goods, Also two oxen, two Cows, and ten sheep & ten
lambs, Also Liberty to keep in my Pasture as my pasture now is three
Cows & one horse perpetualy to him & his heyrs for euer, Provided
he doth not fence perticulerly that land that he hath in the pasture,
and also that he make his proportion of fence to the pasture & do
his part at trenching as need may be Also I giue him one Quarter
part of all the Hides & leather that Do belong to me in the Pitts or
elce where, Farther I giue him one half of the Marsh knowne by the
name of the four acres, Also I giue him the fouling Peice that he
useth & a Musket, ffarther I giue him all the Debts that he hath or
shall make by shoe making except what he hath Done for his owne
Brothers which shall not be by him demanded of them, Also I giue
him eight Rods of Ground which I haue Reserved out of Williams
part where Henry Dole was wont to plant Cabedges all which I giue
to my said son Abner Dole to him & his heyrs for euer, Also I giue
to my said son one quarter part of my Hay Boate and one third part
of my Tooles & utinsills of Husbandry.

To my Daughter Ha͠ah Moodey the wife of John Moodey besids
what I formerly gaue her I giue one eighth part of all my Land both
upland and Marsh in plumb Iland lying Partly in Newbury and
partly in Rowley bounds, also my ffreehold which I Bought of Capt
Nelson & Benjamin Lowle wth all the Priviledges that shall or may
arise therby all which I giue to her and her Heyrs for Euer, ffarther
I giue her one fifth part of all my houshold goods also one halfe of
all my plate also my negro maid named Lucy and this shall be in

3

ffull of her portion having refference to the agreement made wth John Moodey before theyr Marriage.

I^te. To my Daught^r Apphia Coffin the wife of Peter Coffin be-sids what I haue formerly giuen her I now giue her one half of all my plate and seven pounds in good payment to be paid by my execut^rs heerafter named which is in full of her portion.

I do farther giue to my two Daught^rs aboue named viz Hañah Moodey and Apphia Coffin fiue sheets viz 1 p^r of Brins and three liñen sheets also nine diaper napkins and six Brins napkins & nine liñen napkins & two p^r of pillow cases 1 p^r of Brins & the other p^r of Hollands also four Towells & three Table cloaths one of Diaper one of Calecho & one of Brins to be equally diuided between them both.

I^t. I giue to my daught^r in Law Sarah Walker fiue pounds as mony in a good fether bed

Farther my Will is that wheras I haue provided in this my last Will and Testament that my son Abner Dole shall not demand any thing of his owne Brothers for shoes made by him for them in my life time so my will is that his Brothers shall not demand any thing of him for leather that he hath or may receiue of them or me in my life time.

Farther my will is that for my negro servant Grace that at my death she shall haue her freedom if she will accept of it And for my negro servant named Bette my Will is that shee shall serve faithfully and truly wth my son Abner Dole two years after my decease & then she shall be ffree.

All the rest of my estate both Real and personall not disposed of in this my last Will & Testament whither Debts dew to me by Bill bond Booke or otherwise, or any other estate that may appeer to be mine or due to me in Time to come   My Will is that after my Debts and funerall be discharged that the same and every part ther of be eqnaly diuided among my three sons Richard Dole William Dole & Abner Dole

Farther I appoynt my three sons before named viz Richard Dole William Dole and Abner Dole to be the execut^rs of this my last will and Testament heerby revoaking all former Wills of mine.

Also I appoynt my christian ffreinds Coll Daniel Peirce Esqr Tristram Coffin Esqr and my Brother Benjamin Rolfe to be the over-seers that this my last will & Testament be performed

Also my will is that if it should pleas God that I should Dye be-tween seed time and Harvest that then my whole crop of corn both English and Indian be eqnaly divided among my execut^rs they pay-ing the Rates for the upland and housing for that year.

And for the provision that shall be left by me in the house shall be eqnaly divided between Patience my Deer & loving wife and my two sons William & Abner Dole.

And farther for the Annual payment that I am obliged to pay unto

Patience my dear and loving wife by obligation before our Mariage my will is that it shall be paid by my execut^{rs} Anualy some time in the moneth of October

In Wittness to all and singuler the premises I the said Richard Dole sen^r as my last will & Testament haue heer unto set my hand & seale this twenty fifth day of March Año Domi one thousand six hundred ninty & eight and in the tenth year of the Reigne of our Sovereign Lord William the third by the Grace of God of England Scotland ffrance & Ireland King defend^r of the ffaith & 'ca

RICHARD DOLE   Seal

Signed Sealed and
declared by m^r Richard
Dole sen^r to be his last
Will & Testam^t in presens of
us

    Jno Webster juni
    Jona Than grele
    Henry Short

memorandum that ye fiue last lines of ye parragraff belonging to William Dole in this will were cancelled by the desire & order of the Testator on the fifteenth day of September Año Domi 1699 in presens of us wittnesses and the words (& his heyrs foreuer entered in the first line of sd paragraf

Nehemiah Jewet
Tristram Coffin
Henry Short.

Proved 30 July 1705.

WILLIAM BRACKENBURY.

The 24th of July Anno 1668. I William Brakenbury being weak in body but sound of mind & of good remembrance praysed be God, And being mindfull of my disolucon doe make this my Last will & testament in manner following. first I give my soul to God that gave it in & through the Lord Jesus Christ my deare redeemer, And my body to the earth after my decease to be decently interred therein: And for my Temporall Estate which God hath given mee vpon serious consideracons And different from my former Wills I doe dispose as followeth: After my funerall charges & just debts paid, Imprimis I give vnto my Grandsonne Isaack Foster Ten pounds to buy him books.

Item I give unto my Grandsonne John Ridgeway five pounds & a calfe.

Item I give vnto my grandchild Alice Ridgeway five pounds And a this yeares calfe & a ewe lamb.

Item I give vnto all the rest of my Grandchildren fiffty shillings apeice all which Legacys my will is that they shall be paid within halfe a yeare after my decease.

Item I give vnto Alice my wife one third part of all my Lands And Goods for her comfortable support during her naturall life.

Item I give vnto my sonne Samuell And to my daughter Anne Foster and her children And to my daughter Mary Ridgeway And her children the other two parts of all my Lands And goods, to be equally divided between them in thre equall parts: And if they cannot Agre among themselves as to the devession my will is that my overseers hereafter mencõoned shall devide the sayd two parts of my Sayd Estate into thre equall parts And that my sonne Samuell shall choose first which part he will haue: And my daughter Anne Foster shall haue the second choyce and my daughter Mary Ridge-way the third.

Item After my sd wifes deceas my will is that her third part of all my lands & goods, or what remaines thereof, be equally divided between my sonne Samuell my daughter Anne Foster And my daughter Mary Ridgeway as afforsd.

Item I give vnto my sonne in law William Foster And to my sonne in law John Ridgeway fiffty shillings apeice.

Item I give to mr Michall Wigglesworth And to mr Benjã Bunker And to my conzen Richard Brakenbury Ten shillings apeice.

And for the pformance of this my sd will I ordeyne & constitute my sonne Samuell my Executor: And John Sprague Peeter Tufts & John Wayte my ouerseers to whome I give fiue shillings apeice. my true meaning is that my sonne Samuell my daughter Ann Foster & my daughter Mary Ridgeway shall haue the produce of the two third parts of all my estate during my wifes life, And after my sd wifes deceas my whole estate shall then be equally divided between my sonne Samuell my daughter Anne Foster And my daughter Mary Ridgeway as afforsd, to be & remayne for euer to my sd sonne Samuell, & to my daughter Anne Foster & her children & to my daughter Mary Ridgeway & her children. In wittnes wherof I haue hereto sett my hand the day & year abovesd.

In psence of us   WILLIAM BRAKENBURY.
John Reyner junr
Joseph Illes.

Proved 21 September 1668.

JOHN WINSLOW.

In the name of God Amen the twelveth day of March in the yeare of our Lord according to the Computacõn of the Church of England one thousand six hundred seaventy and three Annoq Regni Regis Cař: Secundi Angliæ &c xxvj. I John Winslow senr of Boston in the

Countie of Suffolke in New England Merchant being weake of Body but of sound and perfect memory praysed be Almighty God for the same Knowing the uncertainety of this present life and being desirous to settle that outward Estate that the lord hath lent me I doe make this my last Will and testament in manner and forme following (that is to say) ffirst and principally I comend my soule to almighty God my Creator hopeing to receive full pardon and remission of all my sins and saluation through the merritts of Jesus Christ my Redeemer: And my body to the Earth to be decently buryed with such charges as to the ouerseers of this my last Will and Testament hereafter named shall be thought meet and convenient And as touching such worldly Estate as the lord hath Lent me my Will and meaneing is the same shall be imployed and bestowed as hereafter in and by this my Will is Exprest.

Inprimis I Doe revoake renounce and make voide all Wills by me formerly made and declaire & appoint this my last Will and Testament.

Item. I Will that all the Debts that I justly owe at the time of my decease to any person or persons whatsoever shall be well and truely contented and paid in convenient time after my decease by my Executoʳ or overseers hereafter named. Item I giue and bequeath unto my Deare and well beloved wife Mary Winslow the use of my now dwelling house with the gardens and yards thereunto belonging for and during the tearme of her naturall life. Item I give and bequeath unto my said wife the use of all my houshold goods for her to dispose of as she shall thinke meet. Item I give unto my said wife the sume of ffoure hundred pounds in lawfull mony of New England to be paid unto her by my Executoʳ or overseers hereafter named in convenient time after my decease. Item after the death of my said wife I give and bequeath my said dwellinghouse with all the Land belonging to the same unto my sone John Winslow and to his heires for ever he or they paying when they come to possesse & enjoy the same the sume of ffifty pounds of Lawfull mony of New England unto William Payne the sone of my Daughter Sarah Meddlecott And also to Parnell Winslow Daughter to my son Isaack Winslow the full sume of ffifty pounds of like Lawfull mony: And my Will is that both the said sums be paid into the hands of my overseers to be improved for them untill they come to age or the day of Marriage with the full profitt that they make of the same And in case either of the said Children dye before they come of age or to marriage as afforesaid: My will is that the survivoʳ of them shall then enjoy both the said sums: But in case both of them should dye before they come to age: My Will is that then the said sums shall be Equally divided amongst the Daughtoʳs of my Daughtor Latham to be paid unto them as they come to age or marriage as afforesaid. Item my Will is that my Katch Speedwell (whereof I am the sole owner) and the produce of the Cargo that I sent out in her: be (at her returne to Boston) disposed of by my overseers hereafter named and the neate produce thereof be Equally divided amongst my Children my sone John Winslow onely Excepted and to have no part thereof: Item I giue and bequeath unto my sone Benjamin the full sume of one hundred pounds to be paid him by my Executo^r or overseers hereafter named when he shall attaine the Age of twenty one yeares. Item my Will is that if my sone Edward Winslow shall see cause to relinquish his s^d part and intrest in the s^d Katch Speedwell and her proceeds: then my Will is that he shall have one quarter part of my Katch John's Adventure unto his owne proper use: And then the said Katch and Cargo to be Equally divided among my other Children : my son John Excepted as afforesaid togather with my sone Edward from haveing any part in the afforesaid Katch or Cargo. Item I give and bequeath unto my grandchild Susanna Latham the sume of thirty pounds in mony to be paid her at the day of her marriage And to the rest of my Daughter Lathams Children I give and bequeath unto Each of them five pound p peece to be paid unto them as they shall come to age or the day of marriage. Item I give and bequeath unto my sone Edward Winslows Children the sume of five pounds p peece to be paid unto them as they shall come to age or the Day of Marriage. Item I give and bequeath unto my sone Edward Grey his children that he had by my Daughter Mary Grey the sume of twenty pounds p peece to be paid unto them when they come to age or the day of their respective marriages. Item I give unto my sone Joseph Winslow's two Children five pounds p peece to be paid unto them as afforesaid. Item I give unto my Grandchild Mercy Harris her two Children five pounds apeece to be paid unto them as afforesaid. Item I give and bequeath unto my Kinsman Josiah Winslow now Governo^r of New Plimoth the sume of twenty pounds to be paid unto him by my overseers in Goods: Item I give unto my Brother Josiah Winslow the sume of twenty pounds to be paid unto him by my overseers in Goods: both in convenient time after my decease. Item I give unto my kinswoman Eleano^r Baker the Daughter of my Brother Kenelem Winslow fiue pounds to be paid her in goods by my overseers in convenient time after my decease. Item my will is that what my Estate shall amount unto more then will pay funerall Charges My Debts and Legacyes in this my will given and bequeathed it shall be divided (after the Decease of my said wife) among my seaven Children in Equall proportions Except any one of my said Children shall have any Extraordinary providence befall them by way of any Eminent Losse then that part of my Estate that shall remaine as afforesaid shall be divided & distributed according to the prudence and discression of my overseers hereafter named or any two of them: Item my will is that in case any of my now children shall dye before my said wife that then his or their proportion of the said remaineing Estate shall be disposed to his or their Children if they have any: if not, then that part or parts shall be equally divided amongst the survivors of my said Children : Item I give to Mr Paddyes Widdow five pounds as a token of my love. Item my will is that my Negro Girle Jane (after she hath served twenty yeares from the date hereof shall be free : and that she shall serve my wife during her life and after my wifes decease she shall be disposed of according to the discression of my overseers hereafter named or any two of them : Item I doe nominate and appoint my sone John Winslow the sole Execut^r of this my last Will and testament : Item I doe hereby nominate & appoint my loveing ffriends Mr Thomas Brattle Mr William Tailer and Mr John Winsley my Overseers to see this my will performed so farr as they can : And I doe hereby give unto my said Overseers five pounds apeece in mony as a token of my love Item my will is that my said overseers or any two of them shall & hereby have full power to make saile of any part of my vessell or vesells that I have not hereby disposed of : And also any other goods wares and merchandize for the best advantage of my afforesaid Children : And better paym^t of other Legacyes by me hereby given & bequeathed : Item my will is that during the absence of my said Execut^r my over-seers above named or any two of them have full power to act in all matters and things respecting this my will as if he was personally present : And farther my Will is that my said Execut^r shall not act in any matter or thing respecting this my Will without the advice and consent of my said overseers or two of them And that my Execut^r shall not under any pretence whatsoever claime any more of my Es-tate then I have hereby bequeathed him.   In Witnesse whereof I the said John Winslow sen^r have hereunto set my hand & seale the day and yeare first above written.

Signed sealed & published by John   JOHN WINSLOW   Seal.
Winslow Senr as his last will & Testam^t
in the presence of us
    John Joyliffe
    John Hayward scr.
    Proved 31 July 1674.

MARY WINSLOW.

IN the name of God Amen the thirty first day of July in the yeare of our Lord one thousand six hundred seventy and Six   I Mary Winslow of Boston in New England Widdow being weake of Body but of sound and perfect memory praysed be almighty God for the same Knowing the uncertainety of this present life and being desirous to settle that outward Estate the Lord hath Lent me, I doe make this my last Will and Testam^t in manner and forme following (that is to say) First and Principally I comend my soule into the hands of Almighty God my Creato^r hopeing to receive full pardon and remission of all my sins, and Salvation through the alone merrits of Jesus Christ my redeemer : And my body to the Earth to be buried in Such Decent

manner as to my Execute[r] hereafter named shall be thought meet
and convenient and as touching such worldy Estate as the Lord hath
Lent me my Will and meaneing is the same shall be imployed and
bestowed as hereafter in and by this my Will is Exprest.

Imp[r] I doe hereby revoake renounce and make voide all Wills by me
formerly made and declaire and apoint this my last Will and Testam[t]
Item I will that all the Debts that I Justly owe to any manner of
person or persons whatsoever shall be well and truely paid or ordained
to be paid in convenient time after my decease by my Execute[r]
hereafter named. Item I give and bequeath unto my sone John
Winslow my great square table. Item I give and bequeath unto my
Daughter Sarah Middlecott my Best gowne and Pettecoat and my
Silver beare bowle and to each of her children a Silver Cup with an
handle : Also I give unto my grandchild William Paine my Great silver
tankard : Item I give unto my Daughter Susannah Latham my long
Table : six Joyned stooles and my great Cupboard a bedstead Bedd and
furniture there unto belonging that is in the Chamber over the roome
where I now Lye : my small Silver Tankard : six Silver Spoones, a case
of Bottles with all my wearing apparrell : (except onely what I have
hereby bequeathed unto my Daughter Meddlecott & my grandchild
Susanna Latham :) Item I give and bequeath unto my Grandchild
Ann Gray that trunke of Linning that I have alreddy delivered to
her and is in her possession : and also one Bedstead, Bedd, Boulster
and Pillows that are in the Chamber over the Hall : Also the sume
of ten pounds in mony to be paid unto her within six monthe's
next after my decease : Also my will is that my Execute[r] shall pay
foure pounds in mony p ann for three yeares unto M[rs] Tappin
out of the Intrest of my mony now in Goodman Cleare hands for
and towards the maintenance of the said Ann Gray according to my
agreem[t] with M[rs] Tappin : Item I give and bequeath unto Mary
Winslow Daughter of my sone Edward Winslow my largest Silver
Cupp with two handles : and unto Sarah Daughter of the said Edward
my lesser Silver cupp with two handles : Also I give unto my said Sone
Edwards Children six silver spoones to be divided between them :
Item I give and bequeath unto my grandchild Parnell Winslow the
sume of five pounds in mony to be improved by my Execute[r] untill he come of age : and then paid unto him with the improvem[t] Item
I give & bequeath unto my grandchild Chilton Latham the sume of
five pounds in mony to be improved for him untill he come of Age
and then paid to him with the improvem[t] Item my will is that
the rest of my spoones be divided among my grand children according to the discression of my Daughter Middlecott : Item I give unto
my Grandchild Mercy Harris my White Rugg : Item I give unto
my Grandchild Mary Pollard forty shillings in mony. Item I give
unto my grandchild Susannah Latham my Petty Coate with the Silke
Lace : Item I give unto Mary Winslow Daughter of my sone Joseph
Winslow the sume of twenty pounds in mony to be paid out of

the suṁe my said Sone Joseph now owes to be improved by my Execuᵗᵒʳ for the said Mary and paid unto her when she shall attaine the Age of Eighteene yeares or day of marriage which of them shall first happen. Item I give and bequeath the full remainder of my Estate whatsoever it is or wheresoever it may be found unto my children Namely John Winslow Edward Winslow Joseph Winslow Samuell Winslow: Susannah Latham and Sarah Middlecott to be equally divided betweene them. Item I doe hereby nominate constitute authorize and appoint my trusty friend mʳ William Tailer of Boston afforesᵈ merchant the Sole Execuᵗᵒʳ of this my last Will and testamᵗ: In Witness whereof I the said Mary Winslow have hereunto set my hand and Scale the day and yeare first above written.

Signed Sealed & Published by the above named Mary Winslow as her Last Will & testamᵗ in the presence of us after the adding of foure lines as part of her will.
John Hands
ffrancis H Hacket
her marke
John Hayward scr.
Proved 11 July 1679.

Memorandum I doe hereby also Give and bequeath unto mʳ Thomas Thacher paster of the third Church in Boston the sume of five pounds in mony to be pᵈ in convenient time after my decease by my Execuᵗᵒʳ.

MARY ⅏ WINSLOW
her marke   Seal

INCREASE NOWELL.

The 23 of the 4ᵗʰ Month 1655.

I Increase Nowell of Charlestowne in New England planter being of sound mind and memory (at this present blessed be God) do make & ordaine this my last Will & Testamᵗ.

First. I Commend my soule to Allmighty God my heavenly Father who hath freely loved it, and given his Sonne to redeeme it by shedding his precious blood that he might cleanse it.

2. Next I commit my body to yᵉ ground to be buried in a comely manner if the Lord please.

3. Next my debts Legacies & funerall charges being paid I give my wife a full third of my estate and ten pound over.

4. Next I give my mother Coitmore five pound a small token of my love if living at my death.

5. Next my will is that my sonne Increase, his owne inclination being to Sea, be brought vp a Seaman.

6. Next my will is that my sonne Alexander if he incline to learning be brought up a Scholler, if y° estate be able to beare it, & he prove towardly, & capable, if not in some other honest trade as my Executo^{rs}, & overseers thinke meete.

7. My estate remaining after my debts & legacies are paid, my will is to have it divided into Six parts of which Samuell to have two parts, Increase, Alexander, Mehetabell, & Mary to have each one part, if any of them dye before they come to age, or be married, the survivo^{rs} to have the part belonging to them, my sonnes to have their portions at twenty one yeares of age, or at their marriage with their Mothers Consent which shall be first, my Daughters to have their portions at twenty yeares of age, or at their marriage with their Mothers Consent which shall be first.

9. Next I give to Mr Zachary Sims o^r Pasto^r of Charlestowne forty shillings.

10. Next I give to Mr John Wilson Pasto^r of Boston forty shillings.

11. Next I give to Mr John Green ruling Elder in Charlestowne twenty shillings.

12. Next I give Ralph Mousall forty shillings.

13. Next I give to Robert Hale forty shillings.

Lastly I ordaine, & make my loving Wife Parnell Nowell, & my sonne Samuell Nowell my Executo^{rs}, & Ralph Mousall & Robert Hale my overseers of this my last will & Testam^t in wittnesse whereof I have hereunto set my hand: this 23th of ye 4 M° 1655.

by mee INCREASE NOWELL.

Proved 25 December 1655.

At a County Court held at Charlestowne.

25. ¹⁰⁄_{mo} 1655.

Mr Zachery Simes Pasto^r of the Ch: at Charlestowne, and Sarah the wife of Hugh Williams of Boston. Deposed in Court that the above named Increase Nowell deceased being of sound Judgement & good memory made this above written his last will & testam^t to their best knowledge & vnderstanding.

THOMAS DANFORTH Recorder.

WILLIAM JOHNSON.

I William Johnson being weake in body but of sound memory calling to mind my mortality do make this my last Will & testam^t. flirst I comitt my Soull to God who gave it mee, and my body to the earth therein to be decently buryed after life departed, As for my outward estate I dispose of as followeth, & that after my decease, I do give unto my beloved wife Elizab: Johnson full pow^r to sell my

land on misticke side, lijng neere to the land of John Sergeant, and
my will is that my beloved wife shall pay to my sonne Joseph Johnson Twenty pounds of the first paym^t for the land, and to pay to my
sonne Jonathan Johnson Ten pounds of the first paym^t, and that my
sonne Jonathan Johnson shall receive of his Mother more ten pounds
of the last paym^t for the land, and ye rest of the pay for the land I
give it to my beloved wife. Item I do give to my daught^r Elizab.
Wiar my land at Cambr: line contcyncing foure acc^{rs} more or less,
I give it her & her heyres for ever after my decease. It^m. I do
give to my Grand Child Elizab: Bacon six sheep & lambs now
in her possession. I give it to her after my decease. Itm. I do
give to my sonne Nathaniel Johnson the right & interest that I
haue in the house & land that his wife Joanna Johnson lives in, and
further I give unto him the barne and land belonging to it, adjoync-
ing to ye land belonging to the house of my sonne Nathaniel Johnson. the barne shee is to haue possession of after my wifes decease
& not before. I do give this house land & barne to my sonne
Nathaniel if he be alive, if not then I give it to his two sonnes, they
to possesse it w^t they come to the age of twenty one yeares, and my
daughter Joannah Johnson to injoy it till that time, And for the rest
of my estate of housing lands moveables whatsoever elce that is my
estate, I give it to my well beloved wife Elizab: Johnson for her
comfortable lively hood, and if that shee stand in need of supply I
do give her pow^r to sell any part of the housing or land or the whole
for her comfortable subsistance, and my will is that my well beloved
wife haue pow^r to dispose of my household goods to any of her
children either in the time of her life or at her death as shee shall
see cause, And at my wifes decease my will is that w^t of th' estate
shall then remaine of housing land or moveables undisposed of shall
be divided among my sonnes vizt John Johnson Joseph Johnson
Jonathan Johnson Nathaniel Johnson or his Children if he be dead,
& Zachariah Johnson & Isaac Johnson, my eldest sonne to haue a
double porccon Jno Johnson, the rest of my sonnes to haue equall p^{ts}
of this estate that my wife may leaue at her decease, And further my
will is that my sonne Zachary Johnson should haue the Kill house,
and ye Mill in it, if so much fall to his share, if not he to haue the
house & mill paijng to his Brethren the overplus that they haue
equall shares according to the will, And I do appoynt my beloved
wife my sole Executrix of this my last will & testam^t made the 7th
of decemb. 1677. and in testimony hereof I haue hereunto sett my
hand.

witnes the marks   WILLIAM JOHNSON.
  of Richard Kettle
  Jno Cutler

Proved 2 April 1678.

In the Name of God Amen the Sixth Day of April Ann°
Dom¹ One thousand six hundred Eighty and Eight. I Rebecca
Lynde of Charls-Town in New England Widdow being in perfect
health and of sound and perfect memory (prays be given to Almighty
God for the same) and knowing the uncertainty of this present life and
that all flesh must yeild unto death when it shall please God to call
and being desirous of settling my outward estate before my departure out of this world, Do make and declare this my last will and
testament in manner and forme following (that is to say) First and
principally I comend my sole to Almighty God my creator assuredly
beleaveing that I shall receive full pardon and remission of all my sins
and be saved by the precious death and merits of my savio' and
redemer Christ Jesus, and my body to the earth from whence it
was taken to be buried in such desent manner as to my Ecxecuto'
hereafter named shall be thought meete and convenient, And as
touching such worldly estate as the Lord in mercy hath lent me
my will and meaning is, the same shall be imployed & bestowed as
hereafter by this my will is expressed. Revoking and adnulling by
these presents all Wills heretofore made and declared either by word
or written. And this to be taken for my last will and testamend and
none other. First I will that all those debts and duties that I owe in
right or conscience to any manner of pson or persons whatsoever
shall be well and truly contented and paid within convenient time
after my decease by my Executo' hereafter named and my funerall
expences being discharged the remainder of my estate I give and bequeath as followeth viz'.

Imp^{rs} I Give and Bequeath unto my two Daughters namely
Elizabeth Kemble and Rebecca Jenner All my Household Goods of
what kind soever (except some part of my plate otherwise disposed
of as is hereafter expressed) to be equally diuided between them
and to be to their use and behoofe for ever.

Item I Give and Bequeath unto my Grand-child David Jenner one
Silver Spoon marked R L:

Itt I Give and Bequeath unto my Grand-child Nicholas Trerise
my Silver Tankard marked N R T:

Itt I Give and Bequeath unto my Grand-child Hannah Trerise my
Silver Cupp marked N R T:

Itt I Give and Bequeath unto my Grand-child Elizabeth Jenner
a Silver Cupp marked R T:

Itt I Give and Bequeath unto my Grand-child Mary Goose my
Silver potenger marked N R T:

Itt I Give and Bequeath unto my Grand-child John Goose one
Silver Spoon marked R L:

Itt I Give & Bequeath unto my Daughter Kemble two Silver
Spoons marked R T:

Itt I Give and Bequeath unto my Grand-child Sarah Kemble a Silver Spoon marked I L:

Itt I Give and Bequeath unto my Grand-child Rebecca Lynde one Silver Spoon marked R L.

Itt I Give and Bequeath unto my Grand-sonn John Goose five pounds to be paid him at the age of One and twenty yeares.

Itt: I Give and Bequeath unto my Grand-child Mary Goose the summ of five pounds to be paid her at the age of twenty one yeares or day of marriage either of which shall first happen But if that either of my said Grand-children the above named Mary or John Goose depart this life before the respective time appointed for the payment of their above mentioned Legacies of five pounds p^r piece (which is to be understood are to be paid in current money of new: england) then my mind and will is that the surviveo^r of them shall have obtaine and enjoy the others bequeathed Leagacie of five pounds at the time it should have been paid to the deceased had he or she lived.

Itt. I Give and Bequeath unto my Grand-child Nicholas Trerise All that my Dwellinghouse and land with the wharf & appurtenances thereunto belonging with the liberties & preuiledes to the s^d house & promisses appurtaining Scittuate lying and being in Charls-Town aforesd now or late in the Tenour and occupation of James Kelly and Robert Smith or one of them, which was formerly the estate of Mr Abraham Pratt. Hee the said Nicholas Trerise paying within six months after my Decease unto his Brother my Grand-child John Trerise the full sume of tenn pounds of current money of New: England which sume I hereby bequeath unto the s^d Jno Trerise to be paid as aforesd.

Itt I Give and Bequeath unto Hannah Trerise All that my Smale Dwelling house or Tenement Scituate lying & being in Charls: Town aboves^d with the appurtenances and previledges thereunto belonging in the same manner as 1 now possess the same or of right might or could do which said Tenement was the Dwelling of Good^n Stowres.

Itt 1 Give and Bequeath unto my Sonn m^r Joseph Lynd all my land in and neer the Township of Redding with the appurtenances &c. thereto.

Itt I Give and Bequeath unto my Grand-child m^r David Jenner of Boston Merch^t my Dwelling house in which I now dwell and ground whereon it standeth and land adjoyning Scittuate in Charls-Town above s^d wth all liberties preuiledges easem^{ts} & appurtenances thereunto belonging.

Lastly. I Give and Bequeath unto my good friend Mr Benjamin Bullivant of Boston the Sume of forty shillings to buy him a Ring.

All other my estate whatsoever my just debts & legacies being paid, & funerall expences being discharged as aforesd I Give and bequeath unto my s^d Grand-child m^r David Jenner, whome I appoint

4

constitute & ordaine Sole Executo^r to this my last Will and testament. In Witness whereof I have hereunto put my hand and Seal
the Day and yeare first above written.

The marke of
REBECCA *R L* LYNDE Seal

Signed Sealed and Published
    in the presence of us
    Laur: Hammond
    Abell Beniamin
    Samuell Lord

Proved 17 December 1689.

WILLIAM DOLE.

The Last Will and Testament of William Dole of Newbury in the
County of Essex in the province of the Massachusets Bay in New England which is as followeth,   First in Gods appointed time I Resigne
my soule into the hands of God that gave it, and my body to the
Dust untill the Day of Resurrectyon of the Just, with Good hopes
at that Day to Receeive itt, according to the Gratyous promise of
the God of grace; and Trust In Jesus Christ; and for my Tem-
poral Goods that God hath given me I Dispose of as followeth

I Giue to my Two Sones, Samuel and Benjamin all my Land Leying
on or neere crane neck Knowne by the name of my Rate Lott as it
was Laid out for my Honr^d father Mr Richard Dole Deceased, and
also my Lott of Land Lying on merrimeck River in Newbury; and
also all my Lands and Rights in Lands Leying Ither in Haverhill
Almsbury Salsbury or Rowley and also a piece of marsh Lying in
plumb Island; bounded northerly by my brother abner; and easterly
on the point of sand and southerly partly on my brother Richards
and partly on my brother peters thair marsh: and westerly on the
main Riuer Including the Island in s^d River I also giue to my s^d Two
sones one pair of oxen and Two cows and one horse and a yoak
and chain, all the aboue s^d premises to be equaly Diuided betwixt
them; but if it should please God that Ither Samuel or Benjamin
should Dye with out haires then the aboue mentyoned Lands shall all
be for the suruineing brother.

Itam   I haueing giuen my Daughter Hannah considerable alredy:
I doe ferther giue my s^d Daughter hannah all that her husband did
owe me and also fiue pounds more which is to be in full of her
pourtyō

Itam   I giue to my Daughter Mary soe mutch as will make up
what she haue alredey had the sume of fifty and fower pounds to be
paid with in one year after my Decease;

Itam I Giue to my Daughter Jane soe mutch as will make up
what she hath alredey had, the sume of fifty and fower pounds to be
paid with in one year after my Decease;

Itam I Giue to my Daughter patiance soe mutch as will make
up what she hath alredey had the sume of fifty and fower pounds to
be paid with in one yeare after my Decease;

Itam I Giue to my Daughter apphiah the sume of fifty and fower
pounds to be paid with in one year after my Decease.

Also I Giue to my Dear and Loueing Wife Mary: a lower Roome
and chamber and liberty of a seller; Ither in my Dwelling house or
in the house my sone William liues in which she shall see cause and
also the one half of the household stuff she to have my best bed and
furniture in her part; and also one Quarter part of my money I have
in the house: s^d money and half of my mouables with in Dores I
giue to my s^d beloved wife to dispose of as she shall se cause and
also my marsh Leying in Rowley neere a place called Cow bridg to
Dispose of as she shall se cause: unless one of my sones will giue
her Ten pounds for it; and also the use of a horse when she shall
se cause and also the use of Two cows which shall be kept for her
sumer and winter and also Twelve bushils of Indian corne and Three
of Rye: and one of wheat; and eight bushels of mault and Twelve
pound of sheepswool and eight pounds of cotton wool and eight
pounds of flex to be paid her yearly and Eight cords of wood yearly
to be deliuered at the Dore: and also one Third part of my orchard
and a conveniant garden of two Rods: It is to be understood that
the use of my house and all the yearly payments which I have giuen
my s^d wife, she shall have paid her as is above exprest soe Long as
she shall Reemain my Widdow but if she shall se cause to marrey
again then she shall aquit all her aboue mentioned gifts Excpt the
half of the mouable estat with in Dores and the money and the marsh
aboue s^d and in lieue thareof my Executors shall pay her fourty
pounds money.

Also I giue to my sone William in perticular the house he now
Dwels in and the barne by it: and also a piece of marsh knowne by
the name of the fower acres in Newbury as it Layes Joyning to my
brother Abners marsh also I giue to my sone Richard in perticular
my Dweling house and barne by it.

Lastly I make my Two Sones William and Richard my Whole and
Sole Executors of this my Last will and Testement to Recceive all
my Lands meadows goods and Chattels; that I have not Disposed of
to be Equaly Divided betwixt them; and to Receive all my Debts
y^t is Due to me and to pay all the Debts that I Doe owe and funeral
charges and also to pay all the Leagasies y^t I have given.

My will ferther is that if it should please god to take away my
sone Richard by Death and he leaue no male Hair then my sone
Samuel shall haue what I haue giuen to my son Richard as to housing and Lands, and on the same condityons but I doe order and my

will is y' If my sone Richard Dye and laue a widow and only
Daughters that s⁴ widdow shall Injoy one Third part of the housing
and Lands y' I haue giuen to my sone Richard Dureing her widdow
hood, and my will ferther is y' If my sone Richard Should dye and
leaue only a Daughter or Daughters my s⁴ sone Samuel shall pay
each of them fifty pounds my will is ferther y' If my sone Samuel
(should by the deth of his brother Richard; without male Haire)
come to poses what I haue in Lands giuen to my s⁴ sone; and my
sone benjamin should dye with out haire then my will is y' my sone
william shall haue the one half of the afore s⁴ Rate Lott; and this
is my Last Will and Testement haueing my perfect memory and
understanding as witness my hand and Seale this Twenty ninth Day
of January anno Dom seauenteen hundred and seauenteen or eighteen
                    my will is ferther that my sons
                    Samuel and benjamin shall haue
                    a bed and Ten sheep
    Signed Sealed and declared
in presents of us   The marke **7** and sale
        Siluanus Plumar   of WILLIAM DOLE   Seal
        Samuell Plumer
        Thomas Hale
Proved 11 February 1718.

WILLIAM FOSTER.

    In the Name of God Amen. I William Foster of Charlestowne
in y⁰ County of Midd^x in New England being weak and ill in body,
but of good and p^rfect memory, blessed be God for it And knowing the uncertainty of this life and desirous to settle things in order
Do make Constitute and appoint this to be my Last Will & Testament. Imp^rmis: I Committ my Soul to Almighty God my Creato^r
assuredly beleiving I shall receiue pardon of my sin in and through
Jesus Christ my Dear Redeemer and my body to the earth from
whence it was taken to be decently buried at y⁰ discretion of my
Executo^rs here after named, And as touching such worldly Estate
as y⁰ Lord hath graciously Lent me, my will is it be disposed and
Imployed as hereafter mentioned. First hereby revokeing and makeing voide all and euery other Will or Wills by me heretofore made
by word or writing Do Constitute and appoint this to be my last
Will and Testament and no other. It^m I will that all my Just debts
and duties I ow in right or Conscience to any p^rson whomsoeuer, my
funerall Charges, as also all those Legacies here after named Shall be
well and truly paid in Convenient time after my Decease by my
Executo^rs. Item I Do giue the Improuement of my Dwelling house
Orchard and ground thereto belonging and adjoining, As also my two

peices of Wharfe & Creek and my Wood Lott in y⁰ first Division of Lotts, and Moveables to my beloved wife Ann Foster for her Comfortable Subsistence (till and) so long as She Continueth my Widdow, fully Impowering her with my other Executo⁰ˢ hereafter named to Sell either or both the said peices of Wharf and Wood Lott in y⁰ first Division or moveables for y⁰ better inabling of them to pay my Said Debts and Legacies. Item I do giue and bequeath as follows viz: To My Daughter Mary Phillips I do giue that fifteen pounds to me due from her husband in part of payment for y⁰ Mill, it proving a hard bargaine to him, as also my Second Division of my Wood Lott Lying next or neer Redding. the Same to be to her and her heires for euer. It⁰ I Giue to my Daughter Elisabeth Goose Twenty pounds to be paid her within a Twelvemoneth after my Decease by my Executo⁰ˢ the Same to be to her and her heires for euer. Item I do giue to my Grand Daughter Ann Foster fiue pounds to be paid by my Executo⁰ˢ when She marrieth prouided She marry with y⁰ Consent of her Father and Mother and her Unckle and Aunt Standly other wise She Shall haue no more then any other of my Grand children and the remainder of y⁰ s⁰ fiue pounds to be equally diuided amongst my grand children then Suruiueing. Item I giue to all the rest of my Grand Children fiue Shillings apeice to be paid by my Executo⁰ˢ, to Say, to those that are Ten years of age within a Tweluemoneth after my Decease, and to the rest as they shall arriue at Ten years of age. Item. I do giue to my Kinswoman Elenor Dauis in England* & her daughter Mary Davis Twenty Shillings apeice to be paid within a Tweluemoneth after my Decease. And as for my Dwelling house orchard and Land adjoining as aforesaid at my wifes decease I do give the Same to my two Sonnes Richard Foster and John Foster to be Equally divided detwixt them by two Indifferent men And my Son Richard after such division shall haue his first Choice, & y⁰ same to be to them & theire heires for euer. Further my will is that if my s⁰ Wife shall see Cause to Marry againe she shall then haue but her thirds as y⁰ Law prouides, and y⁰ what remaines at her decease to be divided amongst my Children, to say, y⁰ thirds of y⁰ Housing & Lands to my Said Sons Richard and John, and the Moueables to my other Children then Suruiueing. Further my will is that if any of my Children shall murmur & be dissatisfied with my disposeall of my Estate by this my last will and Testament, that he or they so doeing shall lose the benefit of theire Legacie or Legacies, and the same shall be equally diuided to and amongst those other of my Children that rest satisfied herewith this my Will. It. I Do Constitute and appoint my beloued Wife Ann Foster and my Sonnes Richard Foster & John Foster Joint Executo⁰ˢ of this my last Will & Testament. In Testimony whereof I haue hereunto set my hand & affixed my Seal: May the 7ᵗʰ 1696. Annoq RRⁱˢ Gulielmi 3tii Angliæ &c. octauo.

* This may have been a sufficient address at the time, but now we should like to know more.

Signed Sealed published & declared by m^r Wm Foster
to be his Last will & Testament in p^rsence of us.

    Sam^{ll} Phipps   WILLIAM X FOSTER   Seal
    Tho. Walter   his mark
    Mich^{ll} Brigden
Proved 7 July 1698.

ISAAC WINSLOW.

In the name of God Amen I Isaacke Winslow of New England in
the County of Midlesex being sicke of body but of sound and perfect Memory praysed be to God for it and calling to mind the
uncertaintie of this Transietorie Life and that all flesh must die and
yeald vnto death when it pleaseth God to Call for them and first
being penitent for my sin past desireing forgivenes for the same doe
make this my Last will and Testiement Revocking and Annulling every
will and wills Testiement or Testiements heare to fore by me made
or declared and this to be Taken for my Last will and Testiement
and none other.

first I give and bequeth unto my wife Mary Winslow the house and
Land she now liveth in at Charlestowne in New England. Item
I give that peece of Land Joyning to it to my daughter Parnill
Winslow.   Thirdly I give my part of the Katch Pellican to the
Child my wife went with all when I Left her vpon the twelfe day of
July in Case it Lives if not I give it to my Loveing wife aforesaid.
in wittness whereof I haue hear vnto sent my hand and scalle dated
at Port Royall in Jamaica this twentie sixt day of August In the
year of our Lord one Thousand sixe hundred and seaventy.

    Scalled signed and   ISAACK WINSLOW Seal.
delivered in the presence of
    John Turell
    Thomas P Banfeeld.
    his marke
Proved 30 August 1670.

MARY LONG.

In the Name of God, Amen this fourteenth day of April Annoq
Domini One Thousand Seven hundred and Twenty Annoq RR.
Georgii Magnæ Brittaniæ &c Sexto I Mary Long of Charlestown
in the Countie of Midd^x and province of the Massachusetts bay in
New England (Widow) being weak in body, but of Sound and perfect
mind and memory (thanks be to God) DO make Constitute, ordaine,
and declare this my last will and testament in manner and form following herby revoking and annulling all and every Testament and

Testaments, will, and wills by me hertofore made or declared either by word or writing And this to be taken only for my last will and testament and none other. And first I giue and Comitt my Soul unto Almighty God my Savior & Redeemer in whom and by the merrits of Jesus Christ I trust and beleive Assuredly to be Saved. And my Body to the earth to be buried in such place and manner as shall be found to be my desire manifested in a small scrip of Paper inclosed in this my will. And now for the setling my temporall Estate and such goods, lands, tennements &c. as it hath pleased God far above my deserts to bestow upon mee I Do give order and dispose in manner and form following (That is to say) first I will that all those debts and dues wch I owe in right or Concience to any manner of person or persons whomsoever: Shall be well and truly Contented paid or ordained to be paid within Convenient time after my decease by my Execu^{rs} herafter named.

Item I DO herby Confirme unto my son Samuel Long his heires and Assignes a Dwelling house Comonly Called and known by the name of the great Taverne wth all the land therto belonging, as Expressed and set forth in a deed of Gift under my hand and seal besides what I have given him hertofore.

Item I Give and bequeath unto my Daughter Mary Bradstreet her heires and Assignes forever my now dwelling house with the land therto adjoyning, and garden plot therto belonging with all the privilidges and Appurtanances whatsoever is therunto belonging. As also all my moveable estate plate &c of what name soever & apparrell she being breaved of her sight.

Item I Give and bequeath unto my grandchildren William Welstead and Katherine Welstead of Boston my pasture or mowing ground lying between the land of Joseph Lemon and Samuel Trumball, to them and their heires and Assignes forever wch I vallue at Two hundred pounds.

Item I DO give and bequeath unto my grand Children Richard Foster, Isaac Foster, Parnal Codman, Ann Foster, Sarah Foster and Elizabeth Foster, Simon Bradstreet, Samuel Bradstreet and Mary Bradstreet Five pounds in mony each of them: to be paid unto them within one yeare after my deceace by my Execu^{rs} herafter named.

Item I Give and bequeath unto my four great grand children: vizt Samuel Cary and Richard Carey, Sarah Foster and John Codman each of them forty shillings to be paid as aforesaid, by my Execu^{rs} in Twelve months after my deceace.

All the residue and remainder of my Estate I give and bequeath unto my said son Samuel Long And my daughters Mary Bradstreet Parnall Foster and William Welstead and to their heires and Assignes forever to be Equally divided amongst them. And further my mind and will is And I Do herby ordaine and Appoint my said son Samuel Long and my Daughters Parnal Foster and Mary Bradstreet & my son in Law William Welstead Execut^{rs} of this my last will

and Testament (Having fully sattisfied and discharged the obligation
that my husband John Long of s⁴ Charlestown deceac⁴ was under to
my s⁴ Daughter Parnal Foster formerly Winslow: the same obligation
being Exprest in my s⁴ Husbands last will by me as sole Exeeutrix
therof to be discharged)   Finally my will and meaning is that my
peice of land at Moultens point (as also my marish at yᵉ mill) be
sold by my Exeeuᵗˢ to pay the Debts and Legacies and Funeral
Charges; (the overplus to be Equally divided as aforesaid)   In Witness wherof I have herunto set my hand and Seal declaring the above
written to be my last will and Testament the day and year above
written.

Signed, Sealed and declared   Mary Long   Seal
in presence of us: by the said
Mary Long to be her last will
and Testament.

the words enterlined between the third
and fourth lines from bottom [as also my
marish at yᵉ mill] before signing.
     Eben Austin
     Robᵗ Ward junʳ
     Ben Dowse junʳ

Proved 2 February 1729.

EDWARD WYER.

In the name of God amen: I Edwarde Wiers of Charlestonne in
the county of midelsex in the masathusets coliny in new inglande
being weake of body, but of sounde disposeing memory, prais be given
to God for the same I doe make this my laste will aud testiment in
maner and forme as folocth that is to say first and principally I
resign my soul into the mircifull hans of allmighty God my creator
asuredly hoping through the mirits of my blesed Saviour to obtaine
pardon and remision of all my Sins. and my body I commit
to the earth whence it was taken to be decently buried by the desere-
sion of my exeentrix hearafter named. and as for my worldly goods
and estate that the Lord hath lent me I do dispose as folocth.

imprimis I do giue and bequeath unto my dear and loving wife Elizabeth Wiers my dwelling house and all my lands and houshould
goods and other estate whatsoever for hir proper eus and behofe
during hir life. and I do giue hir full power to sell what land
shee shall see necesary for the discharging of my debts. and when
my wife is dead and decently buried my will is that my estate
bee eqnaly devided to all my children alike and my will is that
if anny of my children dy befor they receue their portion and
leue a child or children behind them that then that childe or

those children shall haue the parte of my estate which hee or shee
should haue had if living. finaly I make my wife Elizabeth Wiers
soule exeekatrix of this my laste will and testimente revoking all
other wills by me heartofor made.   in witues whearof I haue
hearunto set my hand and seal this twentie and seuenth of desem-
ber and in the year of our Lord God one thousand six hundred and
ninety and two.

   signed sealed and published in the presence of

Samuell Adames   EDWARDE WIERS   Seal.
Richard Stratton   his Q marke
Roberte R Scotte.

Proved 11 July 1693.

JOHN COFFIN.

In the Name of God Amen. I John Coffin of Newbury in the
County of Essex New England Yeoman. Being Sensible of My
Mortality but Being at present of a Sound Disposing mind & memory
do make this my Last will & Testament. Committing my Soul to
God through the merits of Jesus Christ, & my body to the Dust In
hope of a Joyful Ressurrection I do Dispose of my worldly Goods
which God has Given me, in the following manner (viz.)

   Impr I Give to my son Nathaniel Coffin Besides what he has
already had, five pounds money to be paid him by my Executors
hereafter Named in one Year after my Decease.

   Item. I Give to my Daughter Abigail Whittemore five pounds
money to be paid her in two Years after my Decease, & also one
Case of Draws & one feather Bed which I now have in my house, to
be Delivered her at my Decease.

   Item I Give to My Daughter Apphia Jones five pounds money to
be paid her in two Years after my decease & also one feather Bed
which I have in my house to be Delivered her at my wifes Decease.

   Item. I Gine to my Sons Peter Coffin & William Coffin all my
Lands in the Towne of Rumford, (formerly Called Pennecook) in
the province of Newhampshire in New England, in Equal halves to
the Said Peter & William & to their Heirs & Assigns forever.

   Item. I Give to my Son Richard Coffin my Sheep pasture which
Land I bought of Dr Somerby.

   Item I Give to my Two Sons Richard Coffin & Samuel Coffin all
the Rest of my real Estate Lying & being in Newbury & Elswhere
Not before Disposed off in this my will in Equal Halves both in
Quantity & Quality to the said Richard & Samuel & to their Heirs
& Assigns forever.

   And I do Constitute & Appoint my Two Sons Richard & Samuel
To be Sole Execcutors to this my will   To Pay all my Just Debts

& Receive all my Just Claims. To pay all the Legacies Given in
this will & my funeral Charges & to Enable my Son Samuel to fulfill his trust as Executor I Give him my Stock of Creatures of all
Kinds Soever & I do Ratifie & Confirm this to be my Last will &
Testament. In Witness whereof I the sᵈ John Coffin have Set to
my hand & Seal this Seventeenth Day of March in the Second Year
of his majestys Reign George the third King &c A.D. 1762 Signed
Sealed Pronounced & Declared by John Coffin to be his last will &
Testament in presenc of us—

    Joseph Coffin   JOHN COFFIN   Seal.
    Stephen Pettingell
    Joshua Coffin.

Proved 11 October 1762.

JOHN HALE.

In the name of God Amen the seventh Day of April 1768. I
John Hale of Newbury in the County of Essex and Province of
The Massachusets Bay in New England, yeoman, Being weeke in
Bodey but of Perfect mind and memory thanks be given unto God.
Therefor Calling unto mind the mortality of my Bodey and Knowing
that it is appointed for all men once to Dye do make and ordain
this my Last will and Testament that is to say Principally and first
of all I give and Recommend my soule into the Hands of God that
gave it, and my Bodey I Recommend to the Earth to be Buried in
decent Christian Burial at the Discretion of my Executor, nothing
Doubting but at the General Resurrection I shall Receve the same
again by the mighty Power of God and as touching such Worldly
Estate wherewith it hath Pleased God to Bless me in this Life I give
demise and dispose of the same in the following manner and forme—

Imprimise. I give and Bequeath to Mary my dearly Beloved
Wife all my Houcehold goods of all sorts Excepting such things as
I shall hereafter dispose of in this my will I also give to my said
Wife the uce and Profite of one third Part of my Real Estate as the
Law Directs and if she Dye my widow she shall have a Decent burial
by my Executer.

Item. I give to my Beloved daughter Patince Coffin three Pounds
money Besids what I have alredey given her in full of her Portion
to be Paid to her by my Executer In Two years after my deceace.

Item. I give to my beloved daughter Mehitabel Clark Twenty
Shilings to be paid to her by my Executer in three years after my
Diseease besids what I have heretofore given her in full of her Por-
tion.

Item. I give to my beloved daughter Elizebath Swett twenty
Shillings to be Paid to her in three years after my Diseeace by my

Executor besides what I have heretofore given her in full of her Portion.

Item. I give to my Beloved sun Nathaniel Hale Three Pound money to be Paid to him in Three years after my Disceace by my Executor. I also give to him a gun besids what I have heretofore given him in full of his Portion.

Item. I give to my Beloved sun John Hale whome I Likewise Constitute make and ordaine my soule Executor of this my will and to his Heirs and asigns all and singuler y° Lands messuages and Tenements that I have in Newbury or Elcewhere I also give to my said sun John all my Personal Estate that I have not alredey Disposed of In this my Will. I also give him all the Just debts that are owing to me his Paying all the Just Debts that I owe the Legeses and my funeral Charges By him freely to be Posessed and Enjoyed and I Do hereby utterly disallow Revoke and Disannul all and Every other former Testament wills Legeacies and Bequests and Executors by me in any wais before named Willed and Bequeathed Rattifying and Confirming this and no other to be my Last will and Testament in witnes whereof I have hereunto set my hand and seal the Day and year above written.

JOHN HALE   Seal

Signed Sealed Published
Pronounced and declared
by the said John Hale
as his Last will and
Testament in the Presence
of us the subscribers.

Simeon Plumer
John Dole jur
Joseph Willet

Proved 28 January 1771.

RICHARD FOSTER.

In the Name of God Amen I Richard Foster of Charlestown in the County of Middlesex in His Majesty's Province of the Massachusetts Bay in New England Esq' being Weak in Body yet of perfect memory, Thanks be to God therefor, Calling to mind the mortality 'of my Body, and Knowing that it's appointed for all men once to Dy, Do make and Ordain This my last Will and Testament, Principaly I Recommend my Soul into the hands of God that gave it hoping for Mercy thro' the Merits of my dear Redeemer, and my Body I Commit to the Dust to be buried with a Decent and Christian Burial (at the discretion of my Executors hereafter named) Firmly believing that at the General Resurection I shall receive the same again by the Mighty power of God, and as Touching such worldly goods and Estate as God hath pleased in his Providence to bless me withall I demise give and dispose of in the following manner.

Imp^r My Will is that all my Just Debts and Funeral Charges be paid and discharged by my Executors hereafter named.

Item. I Give and Bequeath unto my Beloved Wife Parnel (after my Just Debts and Funeral Charges are paid) all my Estate both Real and Personal during her natural life, for her maintenance with liberty to sell or dispose of what part of my personal Estate she shall think fit, and also full power to sell part of my Real Estate as she Think necessary for the use aforementioned, what of my Estate shall remain after my wifes Decease, her Debts and funeral Charges paid, and after its being apprised as near as may be by men upon Oath to the true Value thereof, I Give and dispose of the same in the following manner.

Item. I Give and Bequeath unto my son Richard Foster the sum of Four hundred pounds.

Item. I Give and Bequeath unto my son Isaac the sum of Four hundred pounds.

Item. I Give and Bequeath unto my Daughter Parnel Codman the sum of Forty five pounds.

Item. I Give and Bequeath unto my Daughter Ann Perkins the sum of Thirty nine pounds.

Item. I Give and Bequeath unto my Daughter Sarah Calef the sum of Thirty two pounds.

Item. I Give and Bequeath unto my Daughter Elizabeth McDaniel the sum of Thirty pounds.

Item. I Give and Bequeath unto my Grandsons Samuel and Richard Cary the sum of Thirteen pounds to be Equaly divided betwixt them, and what Remains of my Estate beside the several sums before given and Bequeathed and paid according to the apprisment shall be Divided into seven equal parts To each child one seventh part, and to my two Grandchildren aforementioned one seventh part Equaly between them, But if my Estate should fall short of paying what I now give, Then Each child and Grand child shall abate in proportion to what I now give and also to what my Daughters have had of me at and after their Marriage as money then went, an account thereof is Entered on my Book, and at the foot signed by me.

Item. I Give and Bequeath unto my sons Richard and Isaac Equaly the Property of my Pew in the Meeting house reserving to my Daughters the liberty and priviledge of sitting therein during, their lives.

Furthermore My Will and meaning is That my two sons viz. Richard and Isaac have the remaining part of all my Real Estate after my wifes decease as it is apprised as aforesaid they paying my other Children and Grand children their proportionable part as aforementioned

And I do hereby appoint my Beloved Wife Parnel and my two sons Richard and Isaac to be Executors of this my last Will and Testament, and I do hereby disallow revoke and Disanull all and every other former Will or Testament, Legacies or Bequeasts by me heretofore made or reputed to be made, Ratifying and confirming this and no other to be my last Will and Testament, In Witness whereof I have hereunto set my hand and [seal] this Twenty second Day of January Ann Domini 1735/6 In the Ninth year of His Majestys Reign.

RICH^d FOSTER. Seal.

Signed Scaled Published Pronounced
and Declared by the said Richard
Foster to be his Last will and Testament
in the presence of us who subscribed
our names in presence of said Testator.

Matthew Johnson
Joseph Austin Junr
Joseph Phillips

Proved 14 January 1745.

WILLIAM WYER.

In the Name of God Amen, I William Wyer of Charlestown in the County of Middlesex in New England Esq being in good Health and of sound mind and memory (blessed be God therefor) But mindful of my mortallity and the uncertainty of Life, Do make and ordain this my last Will and Testament in manner following, that is to say, principally and first of all I recommend my Soul to God, thro' the merits & mediation of Christ my only Redeemer, in Hopes of Eternal Life thro' Him, and my Body to the Earth to be buried in a Decent Christian manner at the Discretion of my Executors hereafter named; And as touching such worldly Estate as it hath pleased God to bless me with in this Life I give & dispose thereof as follows, that is to say,

Imp^{rs} I will that my just Debts & Funeral Charges be duly paid by my Executors

Item I give and devise to my son Edward Wyer and to his Heirs and Assigns my mansion House, where I now dwell, with all the Buildings, out houses, Yards, Gardens and Land thereto adjoyning and belonging; and also my Pasture or Lot of Land at Moreton's Point. I also give and bequeath to my son Edward all my Household Furniture of what kind soever, and my three negro men and my negro woman.

Item I give and devise to my son David Wyer and to his Heirs and Assigns the House and Land which I bought of Cookery with

5

the Shop thereon, and the Pasture or Lot of Land which I bought of John Rand and the Heirs of Nathaniel Dowse.

Item I give and devise to my Grandson William Wyer son of my son Thomas Wyer Dec͠ the Pasture or Lot of Land which I bought of Capt: John Rouse and to the Heirs of his Body lawfully begotten, and for default of such Issue, then the same to be & remain to and among all my Children to be equally divided between them. I also give and bequeath to my said Grandson William the Sum of one thousand five hundred Pounds in old Tenor Bills of Credit to be paid to him by my Executors upon his Arrival at the full age of twenty one years.

Item I give and bequeath to my Daughter Eleanor Foster the sum of three thousand five hundred Pounds in Bills of Credit of the old Tenor to be paid to her by my Executors, the one half thereof within one year and the Remainder within two years next after my Decease.

Item I give and bequeath to my Grand Daughter Elizabeth Wyer, Daughter of my son Edward Wyer the sum of two hundred Pounds in Bills of Credit of the old Tenor to be paid to her by my Executors within two years after my Decease, I also give to her my Negro Girl Dinah.

Item I also give and bequeath to all and every the Rest of my Grand Children, not herein before mentioned, that shall be living at the Time of my Decease the sum of one hundred Pounds in old Tenor Bills of Credit to each and every of them to be paid to them by my Executors within two years next after my Decease.

Item I give and bequeath to my Grandson William Foster my Negro Boy Pompy.

Item I give and bequeath to my Grandson Thomas Wyer my Negro Boy Ephraim.

Item I give and bequeath to my Kinswoman Katharine Welch the sum of two hundred Pounds in old Tenor Bills of Credit to be paid to her by my Executors the one half thereof within one year, and the other half within two years next after my Decease. I also give to the s^d Katharine my Negro Boy Coffy.

Item I give and devise to my two sons Edward and David afore-named and to their Heirs & Assigns my Still-House with all the Land & Wharffe thereto adjoyning, the Warehouse, Cooper's shop & Buildings thereon, and also the Stills with the Appurtenances and Implements of what kind or nature soever belonging thereto, with all my Stock appertaining to the Still House at the time of my Decease, to be equally divided between them, they paying & discharging the several Legacies before given & bequeathed in this my Will, at the times limited for payment of them. And as to the Rest of my Estate, which I shall leave at my Decease (not heretofore bequeathed) in Chattles, Cash, Bonds, Notes & Book Debts, and other Estate whether Real or Personal I give and bequeath the same to

my aforesaid two sons Edward Wyer and David Wyer to be equally
divided between them, to enable them to pay my Debts, funeral
Charges, and the Legacies aforesaid.

And I do hereby make constitute and ordain my two sons Edward
& David Wyer Executors of this my last Will and Testament,
hereby revoking and disannulling all former Wills, Testaments,
Bequests and Executors heretofore by me named willed or bequeathed,
ratifying and confirming this & no other to be my last Will &
Testament In Witness whereof I have hereunto set my Hand & seal
this fifteenth Day of January in the twenty first year of His Majesty's
Reign Annoq Domini one Thousand Seven hundred & forty seven.

    Signed sealed published
pronounced & declared by
the afores^d William Wyer Esq
to be his last Will and Testament in the presence of
    us the Subscribers   WILLIAM WYER   Seal.
    Joseph Austin
    Edward Mirick
    Richard Devens

I the aforenamed William Wyer do by this Codicil to my last
Will & Testament aforewritten ratify and confirm the same with
this Alteration or Addition only, That is to say, I do hereby will
give and bequeath to my Daughter Eleanor Foster the sum of five
hundred Pounds in Bills of Credit of the old Tenor to be paid to her
by my Executors, as an Addition to the Legacy of three thousand
five hundred Pounds in the like Bills given her in my said Will, and
to be paid in the like manner, as is order'd for the Payment of that
Legacy.

I do also hereby give & Bequeath to my Grandson William Wyer
aforenamed in my s^d Will the sum of five hundred Pounds in the
Bills aforementioned as an Addition to the Legacy of one thousand
five hundred Pounds in s^d Bills given to him in my said Will, and
to be paid in the like manner as is order'd for the Payment of that
Legacy. In Witness whereof I have hereunto set my hand & Seal
this Ninth Day of June in the twenty first year of His Majesty's
Reign Annoq Dom: 1748.

    Signed sealed published Pronounced
& Declared by the afores^d William
Wyer as a Codicil to & part of his
last Will & Testament in presence of us
(the Day & year last mentioned.)
    Edward Mirick   WILLIAM WYER   Seal.
    Charles Bowers
    Thad Mason.

Be it known to all men by these Presents that Whereas I William Wyer of Charlestown in the County of Middlesex Esq have made and declared my last Will & Testament in Writing bearing Date the fifteenth Day of January Anno Domini one thousand seven hundred and forty seven, as also a Codicil to the said Will on the same sheet of Paper written bearing Date the ninth Day of June Anno Domini Seventeen hundred and forty eight. I the said William Wyer do by this present further Codicil ratify and confirm my said last Will & Testament, and the said former Codicil; and whereas in & by my said last Will & Testament I gave and bequeathed unto my Daughter Eleanor Foster the sum of three thousand five hundred Pounds in old Tenor Bills of Credit, and in the said Codicil (as an addition thereto) I gave and bequeathed unto my said Daughter the sum of five hundred Pounds in the same Bills; I do hereby further give and bequeath unto my said Daughter Eleanor Foster the further sum of five hundred Pounds in the Bills aforesaid, to be paid unto her by my Executors in the manner and at the Time limited for the Payment of the aforesᵈ Bequests to her.

And Whereas in & by my said Will, I gave and bequeathed unto my son Edward Wyer (among other Things) my three negro men and my negro woman; my mind and Will now is, and I do hereby give and bequeath one of my said Negro men Viz^t my Negro man named Quash unto my son David Wyer & to his Heirs and Assigns.

And I do hereby give and bequeath unto the Revd Mr Hull Abbot, and to the Revd Mr Thomas Prentice the Pastors of the Church of the Town of Charlestown the Sum of twenty Pounds apeice in old Tenor Bills of Credit to be paid unto them by my Execu^rs as soon as conveniently may be after my Decease.

And my Will & meaning is that this Codicil as well as the former aforementioned be, and be adjudged to be part & parcel of my said last Will & Testament, and that all Things herein mentioned & contained be faithfully & truly performed, and as fully & amply in every respect, as if the same was so declared & set down in my last Will & Testament. Witness my hand & seal this twenty ninth Day of December in the twenty second year of His Majesty's Reign Annoq Domini 1748.

Signed sealed published
pronounced & declared by the
afores^d William Wyer as a
further Codicil & part of his
  last Will & Testament in
  presence of us   WILLIAM WYER   Seal.
    Edward Mirick
    Richard Devens
    Thad Mason.

Proved 20 February 1749.

NOTES.

The Coffin Family.[*]

THE first of the name, from whom a direct descent can be traced, is NICHOLAS COFFIN of Brixton,[†] Devonshire, England. He died there in 1613, and in his will,[‡] written 12 September and proved 3 November of that year, he mentioned his wife Joan, his sons Peter, Tristram, Nicholas and John, his daughter Anne, and his granddaughter Joan Coffin. He had a brother Tristram Coffin of Brixton, who died in 1601 or 1602, probably childless.

2. II. PETER COFFIN, eldest son of Nicholas, married Joan Thember or Thumber; he died at Brixton in 1628, and in his will, written 21 December, 1627, proved 13 March, 1628, mentioned his six children; his widow came to New England in 1642 with three of her children, and died at Boston, 30 May, 1661. Children, probably born at Brixton:

   i. Tristram, b. about 1605.   3
   ii. John.
   iii. Joan.
   iv. Deborah.
   v. Eunice, b. ———; m. William Butler of Hartford, Conn., who d. in 1648.
   vi. Mary, b.———; m. Alexander Adams of Boston and Dorchester, who d. 15 January, 1678.

3. III. TRISTRAM COFFIN, eldest son of Peter, born about 1605; married Dionis, daughter of Robert Stevens of Brixton; came to

---

[*] See New England Historical and Genealogical Register, XXIV.

[†] The early register of Brixton has unfortunately disappeared, and the oldest volume dates only from 1668.

[‡] No wills of the Deanery of Plympton can now be found earlier than 1600; but the index to earlier wills still exists, and on it are many of Coffins of Brixton and Plympton St. Mary, a neighboring parish, the earliest being of 1564. Nicholas was perhaps son of John Coffin, senior, of Brixton, who died in 1575.

New England in 1642, and after a short rest at Salisbury settled at Haverhill late in that year; in 1647 he moved to Newbury, where he was authorized to keep an "ordinary" and to "retayle wine, paying according to order," and also to run a ferry on the Merrimack between Newbury and Salisbury; about 1654 he moved again to Salisbury, and in 1660 finally settled with part of his family on the island of Nantucket, of which he was commissioned Chief Magistrate by Gov. Lovelace of New York in 1671; he died there 2 October, 1681. Children:

   i. Peter, b. at Brixton about 1630; m. Abigail, daughter of Edward Starbuck of Dover, N. H., by whom he had several children; was Freeman 23 May, 1666; lived at Dover, and was Deputy 1672, 3, 9; moved to Exeter, was Chief Justice of the Superior Court of the Province of New Hampshire, and Councillor 1692–1714; d. at Exeter 21 March, 1715, aged 84.

   ii. Tristram, b. at Brixton about 1632.   4

   iii. ELIZABETH, b. at Brixton ———; m. at Newbury 13 November, 1651, Stephen Greenleaf, as told later; d. at Newbury 19 November, 1678; he d. 31 October, 1690.

   iv. John, b. at Brixton ———; d. at Haverhill 30 October, 1642.

   v. James, b. at Brixton(?) 12 August, 1640; m. 3 December, 1663, Mary, daughter of John Severance of Salisbury, by whom he had several children; lived at Nantucket, and was Chief Justice of the Court of Common Pleas; d. 28 July, 1720.

   vi. Deborah, b. at Haverhill 15 November, 1642; d. 8 December, 1642.

   vii. Mary, b. at Haverhill 20 February, 1645; m. Nathaniel Starbuck of Nantucket; d. 13 September, 1717; he d. 6 June, 1719.

   viii. John, b. at Haverhill(?) Newbury 13 October, 1647; m. Deborah, daughter of Joseph Austin, by whom he had several children; lived at Nantucket; d. at Edgartown 5 September 1711; she d. 4 February, 1718.

   ix. Stephen, b. at Newbury 11 May, 1652; m. Mary, daughter of George Bunker of Nantucket, by whom he had several children; d. 18 May, 1734; she d. in 1724.

4. IV. TRISTRAM COFFIN, second son of Tristram, born probably at Brixton about 1632; married at Newbury 2 March, 1653, Judith, daughter of Edmund Greenleaf, widow of Henry Somerby; was in 1666 a signer of the document, which Dr. Palfrey unjustly, in my opinion, calls the "unpatriotic petition"; was Freeman of the Colony of Massachusetts 29 April, 1668, and Lieutenant of the second company of Newbury 16 May, 1683; was Representative to the General Court 1695, 1700, 1, 2, and was Deacon of the Church of Newbury twenty years; he died 4 February, 1704, aged 71; she died 15 December, 1705. His will is printed page 11. Children, born at Newbury:

   i. Judith, b. 4 December, 1653; m. 19 November, 1674, John Sanborn of Hampton, N. H.; he d. 10 November, 1723.

   ii. Deborah, b. 10 November, 1655; m. 31 October, 1677, Joseph Knight of Newbury; he d. 29 January, 1723.

iii. Mary, b. 12 November, 1657; m. 31 October, 1677, Joseph Little of Newbury; d. 28 November, 1725; he d. 27 January, 1737.
iv. James, b. 22 April, 1659; m. 16 November, 1685, Florence, daughter of Horace Hook of Newbury, by whom he had several children; d. 4 March, 1736; she d. 6 June, 1712.
v. John, b. 8 September, 1660; d. 13 May, 1677.
vi. Lydia, b. 22 April, 1662; m. Moses Little of Newbury; he d. 8 March, 1691, and she m. secondly, 18. March, 1695, John Pike of Newbury; he d. 13 August, 1714.
vii. Enoch, b. 21 January, 1664; d. 12 November, 1675.
viii. Stephen, b. 18 August, 1665; m. 8 October, 1685, Sarah, daughter of John Atkinson of Newbury, by whom he had several children; d. 31 August, 1725; she d. 20 January, 1725.
ix. Peter, b. 27 July, 1667; m. Apphia, daughter of Richard Dole of Newbury, by whom he had several children; lived at Gloucester; d. at Newbury 19 January, 1747; she d. 14 April, 1725.
x. Nathaniel, b. 26 March, 1669. 5

5. V. NATHANIEL COFFIN, youngest child of Tristram, born at Newbury 26 March, 1669; married 29 March, 1693, Sarah, daughter of Samuel Brocklebank of Rowley, widow of Henry Dole of Newbury; was Deacon of the Church of 'Newbury, and in 1711 was chosen Town Clerk; was Representative to the General Court 1719, 20,·1; was a Councillor of the Province 1730, and a special Justice of the Court of Common Pleas for Essex 1734; he died 20 February, 1749; she died 20 April, 1750. Children, born at Newbury:

i. John, b. 1 January, 1694. 6
ii. Enoch, b. 7 February, 1696; Harvard College, 1714, Rev.; m. 5 January, 1716, Mehitable Moody, by whom he had four children, who all d. young; d. 7 August, 1728; she d. 29 December, 1763.
iii. Apphia, b. 9 June, 1698; d 8 October, 1715.
iv. Brocklebank Samuel, b. 24 August, 1700; Harvard College 1718, Rev.; d. 14 June, 1727.
v. Joseph, b. 30 December, 1702; m. 15 July, 1725, Margaret, daughter of Benjamin Morse of Newbury, by whom he had several children;* d. 12 September, 1773; she d. 9 February, 1775.
vi. Jane. b. 5 August, 1705; m. 2 November, 1729, John Webster of Newbury; d. 19 May, 1783.
vii. Edmund, b. 19 March, 1708; m. at Kittery 15 November, 1732, Shuah Bartlett, by whom he had several children; d. 29 January, 1789.
viii. Moses, b. 2 June, 1711; m. 28 November, 1732, Anna, daughter of William Dole of Newbury, by whom he had several children; d. 22 February, 1793.

6. VI. JOHN COFFIN, eldest son of Nathaniel, born at Newbury 1 January, 1694; married 22 April, 1713, Judith, daughter of Edmund Greenleaf of Newbury; died 30 September, 1762; she

* The Rev. Paul Coffin, D. D., of Buxton, Me., was a son; and among their descendants were the Rev. Charles Coffin, D.D., the Rev. Ebenezer Coffin, Robert S. Coffin the self-styled Boston Bard, and Joshua Coffin the antiquary and historian of Newbury.

died 10 February, 1772. His will is printed page 41. Children, born at Newbury:

 i. Richard, b. 22 November, 1713; m. 30 November, 1738, Abigail, daughter of Joseph Hale of Newbury, by whom he had several children; d. 9 March, 1773; she d. 19 August, 1799.

 ii. Nathaniel, b. 7 September, 1716.   7

 iii. Abigail, b. 8 November, 1718; m. 2 February, 1744, Rev. Aaron Whittemore of Pembroke, N. H.; d. 11 May, 1803; he d. 16 November, 1767.

 iv. Mary, b. 23 July, 1720; d. 25 November, 1737.

 v. Peter, b. 11 May, 1722; m. 6 July, 1769, Rebecca Haselton of Chester, N. H., by whom he had several children; d. at Boscawen, N. H., 15 December, 1789.

 vi. Apphia, b. 13 April, 1724; m. 8 May, 1746, Ichabod Jones of Falmouth.

 vii. William, b. 3 July, 1726; m. 28 March, 1754, Sarah Haselton of Chester, N. H., by whom he had several children; d. at Concord, N. H., 18 October, 1815; she d. 26 May, 1829.

 viii. Samuel, b. 23 November, 1728; m. 27 May, 1752, Anna Pettingill, by whom he had one son; he m. secondly 17 June, 1777, Lydia Bartlett; d. 29 June, 1818; she d. 29 August, 1821.

 ix. ———, son, b. ———; d. infant.

 x. Judith, b. 3 September, 1732; d. 2 November, 1737.

 xi. Sarah, b. 26 September, 1735; d. 1 November, 1737.

7. VII. NATHANIEL COFFIN, second son of John, born at Newbury 7 September, 1716; married 1 March, 1739, Patience, daughter of John Hale of Newbury; settled in 1738 at Falmouth, now Portland, Me., as a physician, and during his whole life enjoyed a high reputation and a large practice; died 12 January, 1766;* she died 31 January, 1772. A short notice of him may be read in the "AMERICAN MEDICAL BIOGRAPHY," by James Thacher, M.D. Children, born at Falmouth:

 i. Nathaniel, b. 20 December, 1739; d. 20 December, 1739.

 ii. Sarah, b. 21 July, 1741; d. in 1826.

 iii. Nathaniel, b. 20 April, 1744.   8

 iv. Dorcas, b. 15 September, 1746; d. 27 June, 1749.

 v. Jeremiah Powell, b. 23 October, 1748.

 vi. Dorcas, b. 20 October, 1751; m. 27 November, 1769, Thomas Colson of Bristol, England; d. in 1801.

 vii. Francis, b. 28 August, 1753; Consul of the United States at Dunkirk, France, where he d. 14 May, 1795.

 viii. Mary, b. 6 October, 1756; m. Samuel Juie Marchant, who d., and she m. secondly, in 1796, Charles Joseph Harford of Stapleton, Gloucestershire, England; d. in 1798.

8. VIII. NATHANIEL COFFIN, eldest son of Nathaniel, born at

---

* We hear from Falmouth, Casco Bay, that on Lord's Day the 12th Instant, departed this Life, of a Paralytic Disorder Dr. *Nathaniel Coffin*, of that Place, Physician, in the 50th Year of his Age.—As his Skill in Physic and Chirurgery had gain'd him a great Acquaintance, so his Death is esteem'd a great Loss in and about that Part of the World.—*Boston Gazette, and County Journal*, 27 January, 1766.

Falmouth 20 April, 1744; married at Charlestown 30 October, 1769, Eleanor, daughter of Isaac Foster of Charlestown; was a very distinguished physician of Portland; received the honorary degree of M.D. from Bowdoin College, 1821; died 18 October, 1826; she died 8 September, 1822. A most favorable notice of him was printed in the Boston Medical Intelligencer, and a memoir of his life, with portrait, may be seen in the book named in connection with his father. Children, born at Portland:

i. Harriot. b. in August, 1770; d. 15 January, 1774.
ii. Mary Foster, b. 21 April, 1772; m. 4 July, 1792, Eben Mayo of Portland; d. 4 February, 1793; he d. 12 September, 1840.
iii. Susanna, b. 4 June, 1773; m. 29 October, 1791, William Codman of Boston; d. 21 April, 1854; he d. in New York, 8 December, 1816.
iv. Harriot, b. 14 May, 1775.   9
v. William Foster, b. 4 February, 1777; d. 5 January, 1788.
vi. Eleanor, b. 22 July, 1779; m. 12 December, 1801, John Derby of Salem; d. in Boston 30 March, 1859; he d. at Salem 25 November, 1831.
{ Francis, b. 16 November, 1780; d. in Boston 18 August, 1842.
{ Thomas, b. 16 November, 1780; m. in Moscow, Russia, about 1829, Ann, dau. of —— Canally of Ireland, widow of John Toal, by whom he had one daughter; d. at Perovo, Russia, in 1832; she d. in Moscow in 1865.
ix. Martha, b. 11 April, 1783; m. 23 September, 1800, Richard Crowninshield Derby of Boston; d. 24 November, 1832; he d. in Philadelphia 4 April, 1854.
x. Nathaniel, b. 11 May, 1785; d. 18 December, 1787.
xi. Isaac Foster, b. 28 March, 1787; Bowdoin College 1806; m. at New Bedford 31 May, 1845, Martha Ann, daughter of John Prince of Jamaica Plain; d. at West Roxbury 24 January, 1861; she d. in Boston 7 September, 1877.

9. IX. HARRIOT COFFIN, fourth child of Nathaniel, born at Portland 14 May, 1775; married at Portland 23 November, 1799, Jesse Sumner of Boston; died in Boston 3 November, 1862; he died 13 October, 1847. Their second child, but eventual sole heiress, HARRIOT COFFIN SUMNER, married the Hon. Nathan Appleton of Boston, and was mother of the author.

The Brocklebank Family.[*]

Jane Brocklebank, a widow with two sons, Samuel and John, settled at Rowley about 1639. They probably came from the neighborhood of Hull, Yorkshire, England, where the name was quite common; but careful research has as yet failed to positively identify her husband. She died at Rowley, in December, 1668.

John Brocklebank, younger son of Jane, married at Rowley 26 September, 1657, Sarah Woodman, by whom he had several children; he died in April, 1666, leaving only two daughters.

2. II. SAMUEL BROCKLEBANK, elder son of Jane, born about 1627; married at Rowley 18 May, 1652, Hannah ———; 29 March, 1653, he was presented to the County Court of Essex at Ipswich "for wearing silver lace," and "confest it, but in considderation of his Imploym[t] & other considderations is discharged of it"; he was a military man, in 1671 Lieutenant, and 15 October, 1673, appointed Captain of the company at Rowley, and was Deacon of the Church 1666–1676; he was killed in the battle with Indians at Sudbury, in April, 1676, aged 48; his widow married 4 March, 1679, Richard Dole of Newbury, and died 6 September, 1690. Children, born at Rowley:

    i. Samuel, b. 28 November, 1653; m. 22 November, 1681, Elizabeth Plats of Rowley, by whom he had children.
    ii. Francis. b. 26 September. 1655; d. in July, 1660.
    iii. Hannah, b. 28 March, 1659; m. 9 June, 1680, John Stickney of Rowley; d. 23 April, 1749; he d. in 1709.
    iv. John, b ———; d. in July, 1660.
    v. MARY, b. ———; m. at Newbury 13 October, 1684, William Dole, as told later; he d. 31 January, 1718.
    vi. Elizabeth, b. ———; m. 14 March, 1686, John Todd of Rowley; d. 5 April, 1725; he d. 21 February, 1741.
    vii. Sarah, b. 29 October, 1666; d. in February, 1667.
    viii. Sarah, b. 7 July, 1668.   3
    ix. Jane, b. 31 January, 1671; m. at Newbury 26 January, 1693, Abiel Somerby of Newbury; d. 26 July, 1728; he d. 8 January, 1744.
    x. Joseph, b. 28 November, 1674; m. 18 February, 1702, Elizabeth Barker of Rowley, by whom he had children; d. 21 April, 1748; she d. 21 November, 1722.

3. III. SARAH BROCKLEBANK, eighth child of Samuel, born at Rowley 7 July, 1668; married at Newbury 3 November, 1686, Henry Dole, who died 13 September, 1690, and she married secondly 29 March, 1693, Nathaniel Coffin; died 20 April, 1750; he died 20 February, 1749.

---

* See Essex Institute Historical Collections, XX.

THE GREENLEAF FAMILY.[*]

EDMUND GREENLEAF, with wife Sarah and several children, came to New England before 1638, and settled at Newbury. Researches made in England by the late Horatio G. Somerby render it certain that he came from Ipswich in Suffolk. His baptism has not been found, but he was quite possibly son of Edmund Greenleaf of the parish of St. Mary-at-the-Tower. He was made Freeman of the Colony of Massachusetts, 13 March, 1639, and the same year was appointed Ensign of the company at Newbury, and permitted to keep a house of entertainment; in 1642 he was Lieutenant, and was appointed "to end small business in Neweberry": in 1647 he was, at his own request, discharged from his military office, and later moved to Boston, where his wife died 18 January, 1663; he married, secondly, Sarah, daughter of Ignatius Jurdaine of Exeter, England, widow first of ———— Wilson, second of William Hill of Fairfield, Conn.; he died ? 24 March, 1671. His will is printed page 1. Children, born at Ipswich, England:

i. Enoch, bapt. at St. Mary-at-the-Tower, 1 December, 1613; bur. at St. Margaret's 2 September, 1617.
ii. Samuel, b. ————; bur. at St. Margaret's 5 March, 1627.
iii. Enoch, b. ————; m. Mary ————, by whom he had several children; lived at Malden and Boston.
iv. Sarah, bapt. at St. Margaret's 26 March, 1620; m. William Hilton of Newbury; d. about 1655; he d. at Charlestown 7 September, 1675.
v. Elizabeth, bapt. at St. Margaret's 16 January, 1622; m. Giles Badger of Newbury; he d. 10 July, 1647, and she m. secondly 10 February, 1649, Richard Brown of Newbury; he d. 26 April, 1661.
vi. Nathaniel, bapt. at St. Margaret's 27 June, 1624; bur. 24 July, 1634.
vii. JUDITH, bapt. at St. Margaret's 29 September, 1626; m. Henry Somerby of Newbury; he d. 2 October, 1652, and she m. secondly 2 March, 1653. Tristram Coffin of Newbury, as told page 50; d. 15 December, 1705; he d. 4 February, 1704.
viii. Stephen, bapt. at St. Margaret's 10 August, 1628.   2
ix. Daniel, bapt. at St. Margaret's 14 August, 1631; d. at Newbury 5 December, 1654.

2. II. STEPHEN GREENLEAF, fifth but second surviving son of Edmund, born at Ipswich, England, in 1628: married at Newbury 13 November, 1651, Elizabeth, daughter of Tristram Coffin; in 1670 was appointed Ensign of the company at Newbury, and in 1685 Lieutenant; was Deputy to the General Court 9 August, 1676, and 13 May, 1686, to the Council of Safety 1689, and to the General Court 1689, '90; his wife died 19 November, 1678, and he married secondly 31 March, 1679, Esther, daughter of Nathaniel Weare of

Hampton, widow of Benjamin Swett of Hampton; was a Captain in the disastrous expedition against Canada in 1690, and was drowned off Cape Breton 31 October, 1690; she died at Newbury 16 January, 1718. His will is printed page 13. Children, all by first wife:

    i. Stephen, b. at Newbury 15 August, 1652; soldier in 1675–6; Captain; m. 23 October, 1676, Elizabeth, daughter of William Gerrish of Newbury, by whom he had several children; she d. 5 or 13 August, 1712, and he m. secondly, in 1713, Mrs. Hannah Jordan of Kittery; d. 30 September, 1743.

    ii. Sarah, b. at Newbury 18 October, 1655; m. 7 June, 1677, Richard Dole of Newbury; d. 1 September, 1718; he d. 1 August, 1723.

    iii. Daniel, b. at Boston 17 February, 1658; d. young.

    iv. Elizabeth, b. at Newbury 5 April, 1660; m. 24 September, 1677, Thomas Noyes of Newbury; he d. in 1730.

    v. John, b. at Newbury 21 June, 1662; m. 12 October, 1685, Elizabeth Hills of Newbury, by whom he had several children; she d., and he m. secondly, 13 May, 1716, Lydia, daughter of Charles Frost of Kittery, widow of Benjamin Pierce of Newbury; d. 24 June, 1734; she d. 13 May, 1752.

    vi. Samuel, b. at Newbury 30 October, 1665; m. 1 March, 1686, Sarah, daughter of John Kent of Newbury, by whom he had children; d. 6 August, 1694; she m. secondly, 28 April, 1696, Peter Toppan of Newbury.

    vii. Tristram, b. at Newbury 11 February, 1668; m. 12 November, 1689, Margaret Piper of Newbury, by whom he had several children; d. 13 September, 1742.

    viii. Edmund, b. at Newbury 10 May, 1671.   3

    ix. Judith, b. at Newbury 23 October, 1673; d. 19 November, 1678.

    x. Mary, b. at Newbury 6 December, 1676; m. in 1696, Joshua Moody of Newbury.

3. III. EDMUND GREELEAF, youngest son of Stephen, born at Newbury 10 May, 1671; married 2 July, 1691, Abigail, daughter of Abiel Somerby of Newbury; died? in 1740. Children, born at Newbury:

    i. Judith, b. 15 December, 1692.   4

    ii. Abigail, b. 6 March, 1695.

    iii. Mary, b. 10 September, 1697.

    iv. Rebecca, b. 22 February, 1700; d. 29 September. 1702.

    v. Edmund, b. 10 February, 1702; m. 4 March, 1725, Mary, daughter of Joseph Hale of Newbury; d. in 1754.

    vi. Henry, b. 22 July, 1705.

    vii. Rebecca, b. 5 November, 1707; d. 19 August, 1709.

    viii. Richard, b. 11 May, 1710.

    ix. Rooksby, dau., b. 11 May, 1713; m. 21 April, 1738, John Clark of Kings Towne.

4. IV. JUDITH GREENLEAF, eldest child of Edmund, born at Newbury 15 December, 1692; married 22 April, 1713, John Coffin of Newbury; died 10 February, 1772; he died 30 September, 1762.

THE SOMERBY FAMILY.

This family is traced back with certainty to HENRY SOMERBY of Little Bytham, Lincolnshire, England, who died in 1609, leaving widow Margaret, and son RICHARD SOMERBY, who died at Little Bytham 1 March, 1639; his children were:

> i. Anthony, bapt. at Little Bytham 16 August, 1610.   3
> ii. Henry, bapt. at Little Bytham 17 March, 1612; came to New Eng-
> land in 1639, and settled at Newbury; Freeman 18 May, 1642;
> m. Judith, daughter of Edmund Greenleaf of Newbury, by whom
> he had four children, of whom two daughters became his eventual
> coheirs; d. 2 October, 1652; she m. secondly 2 March, 1653,
> Tristram Coffin of Newbury, and d. 15 December, 1705.

3. III.   ANTHONY SOMERBY, elder son of Richard, born at Little Bytham in 1610; graduated at Clare Hall, Cambridge, 1635; came to New England in 1639, and settled at Newbury; m. Abigail ———; was Freeman of the Colony of Massachusetts 18 May, 1642; was for some time schoolmaster at Newbury, and in 1647 was appointed Clerk of the Writs as well as Town-clerk; was a signer of the petition of 1666; he died 31 July, 1686; she died 3 June, 1673. His will is printed page 2.   Child:

> i. Abiel, b. at Newbury 8 September, 1641.   4

4. IV.   ABIEL SOMERBY, only child of Anthony, born at Newbury 8 September, 1641; married 13 November, 1661, Rebecca, daughter of Richard Knight; was a signer of the petition of 1666; Freeman 19 May, 1669; died 27 December, 1671; she married secondly, 28 April, 1691, Nicholas Wallis of Ipswich, and died? in 1719.   Children, born at Newbury:

> i. Henry, b. 13 September, 1662; m. 26 June, 1683, Mary, daughter
> of Samuel Moody of Newbury; d. 24 November, 1723.
> ii. Elizabeth, b. 20 December, 1664; m. 29 March, 1683, Daniel
> Moody of Newbury.
> iii. Abiel, b. 21 August, 1667; m. 26 January, 1693, Jane, daughter of
> Samuel Brocklebank of Rowley, by whom he had several chil-
> dren; d. 8 January, 1744; she d. 26 July, 1728.
> iv. Abigail, b. 25 January, 1670.   5
> ⎧ Anthony, b. 12 June, 1672, (posthumous); m. in 1696, Elizabeth,
> ⎪   daughter of Edward Heard of Ipswich, by whom he had several
> ⎨   children; d. 16 September, 1759.
> ⎩ Rebecca, b. 12 June, 1672, (posthumous); m. John Kent of New-
>   bury.

5. V.   ABIGAIL SOMERBY, fourth child of Abiel, born at Newbury 25 January, 1670; married 2 July, 1691, Edmund Greenleaf.

6

The Knight Family.

Among the passengers from Southampton, England, for New England by the "James" in April, 1635, were

John Knight ⎱ of Romsey
Richard Knight ⎰ taylers.

They were undoubtedly cousins. John Knight was either son of Nicholas, and born in 1601, or son of John, and born in 1602; he settled at Newbury; was Freeman 25 May, 1636, and had wife Elizabeth, who died 20 March, 1645; he m. secondly, Ann, widow of Richard Ingersoll of Salem, and died in May, 1670, leaving son John.

RICHARD KNIGHT was son of WILLIAM of Romsey, and was baptized there 14 January, 1603; according to Joshua Coffin he married Agnes Coffley;* he settled at Newbury; was Freeman of the Colony of Massachusetts 25 May, 1636; the same year was chosen one of the first "seven" or selectmen of Newbury, and was for many years Deacon of the Church there; in 1645 he was appointed by the General Court with Edward Woodman and John Lowle "to end small causes under 20ˢ in Neweberry"; 27 September, 1653, his wife being presented to Ipswich Court "for waring a silke hood, upon pᶠes yᵗ her husband is worth abouc 200ˡⁱ is discharged of her pʳsentment"; he was a signer of the petition of 1666; died 4 August, 1683; she died 22 March, 1679. His will is printed page 4. Children:

    i. ANN, b. probably at Romsey; m. 8 October, 1648, Henry Jaques of Newbury, as told later; d. 22 February, 1705; he d. 24 February, 1687.

    ii. Elizabeth, b. ———; m. 8 May, 1660, Anthony Morse of Newbury; d. 29 July, 1667; he d. 25 February, 1678.

    iii. Rebecca, b. at Newbury 3 March, 1643.   2

    iv. Sarah, b. at Newbury 23 March, 1647; m. 20 May, 1663, John Kelly of Newbury; he d. 21 March, 1718.

2. III. REBECCA KNIGHT, third daughter of Richard, born at Newbury 3 March, 1643; married 13 November, 1661, Abiel Somerby of Newbury; he died 27 December, 1671, and she married secondly, 28 April, 1691, Nicholas Wallis of Ipswich; died? in 1719.

---

* Coffley is the name of a family of Romsey, but I could not find this marriage on the parish register; Coffin may however have obtained it from some one of the Knight family.

THE HALE FAMILY.*

Recent searches for the ancestry of Thomas Hale of Newbury have fortunately been successful. The record begins with THOMAS HALE of Watton-at-Stone, Hertfordshire, England, who married Joan Kirby of Little Munden, Herts., and was buried at Watton 19 October, 1630; she married secondly John Bydes of Little Munden. Children, born at Watton:

    i. Dionis, bapt. 15 August, 1602; m. 29 September, 1624, Henry Beane.
    ii. Thomas, bapt. 15 June, 1606.   2
    iii. Mary, bapt. 8 October, 1609; ? m. ——— Whale.
    iv. Dorothy, bapt. 28 March, 1613.
    v. Elizabeth, bapt. 31 August, 1617.

2. II. THOMAS HALE, only son of Thomas, born at Watton-at-Stone in 1606; married Thomasine ———; lived a few years at Watton; came to New England in 1637, and is found at Newbury in 1638; was Freeman of the Colony of Massachusetts 7 September, 1638; moved in 1645 to Haverhill, where he was one of the Commissioners to end small causes, and lived till 1652; then at Newbury till 1657; then at Salem till 1661, when he returned to Newbury; was a signer of the petition of 1666, and died at Newbury 21 December, 1682; she died 30 January, 1683. Children:

    i. Thomas, bapt. at Watton 18 November, 1633; m. at Salem 26 May, 1657, Mary, daughter of Richard Hutchinson of Salem, by whom he had several children; d. at Newbury 22 October, 1688; she m. secondly at Boxford 5 February, 1695, William Watson of Boxford; d. 8 December, 1715.
    ii. John, bapt. at Watton 19 April, 1635.   3
    iii. Samuel, b. at Newbury 2 February, 1640; ? m. 19 March, 1669, Lydia Musgrave, who d. soon, and he m. 21 July, 1673, Sarah, daughter of William Ilsley of Newbury, by whom he had two daughters; moved to Woodbridge, New Jersey; d. there 5 November, 1709; she d. 16 January, 1681.
    iv. Applia, b. at Newbury in 1642; m. 3 November, 1659, Benjamin Rolfe of Newbury; d. 24 December, 1708; he d. 10 August, 1710.

3. III. JOHN HALE, second son of Thomas, born at Watton-at-Stone in 1635; married at Newbury 5 December, 1660, Rebecca, daughter of Richard Lowle; she died 1 June, 1662, and he married secondly 8 December, 1663, Sarah, daughter of Henry Somerby; she died 19 June, 1672, and he married thirdly, Sarah† ———; had the title of Serjeant; died 2 June, 1707; she died 19 January, 1700. Children, born at Newbury:

    i. John, b. 2 September, 1661.   4

---

* See Genealogy of Descendants of Thomas Hale, Albany, 1889.
† She is said to have been a widow Cottle, but her father has not yet been identified; perhaps her first husband was William Cottle.

ii. Samuel, b. 15 October, 1664; d. 15 May, 1672.
iii. Henry, b. 20 October, 1666; m. 11 September, 1695, Sarah, daughter of John Kelly of Newbury, by whom he had several children; d. 21 October, 1724; she d. 10 February, 1741.
iv. Thomas, b. 4 November, 1668; probably d. unmarried.
v. Judith, b. 5 July, 1670; m. 24 November, 1692, Thomas Moody of Newbury; died? in 1757; he d. in 1737.
vi. Joseph, b. 24 November, 1674; m. 25 December, 1699, Mary, daughter of Caleb Moody of Newbury, by whom he had several children; d. 24 January, 1755; she d. 16 April, 1753.
vii. Benjamin, b. 11 August, 1676; d. 31 August, 1677.
viii. Moses, b. 10 July, 1678; Harvard College 1699, Rev.; was minister of Byfield Parish, Newbury; m. in 1703 Elizabeth, daughter of Richard Dummer of Newbury; she d. 15 January, 1704, and he m. secondly Mary, daughter of William Moody of Newbury, by whom he had several children; d. 16 January, 1744; she d. 17 July, 1757.

4. IV.   John Hale, eldest son of John, born at Newbury 2 September, 1661; married 16 October, 1683, Sarah, daughter of Henry Jaques; died 4 March, 1726.   Children, born at Newbury:

i. Rebecca, b. 18 February, 1685; m. in 1703 Jonathan Poor of Newbury; he d. 30 June, 1742, and she m. secondly, 27 December, 1742, Jonathan Jewett of Rowley; d. 16 March, 1760; he d. 26 July, 1745.
ii. John, b. 24 June, 1686.   5
iii. Richard, b. 21 September, 1688; d. 29 September, 1688.
iv. Henry, b. 28 August, 1689; d. 2 February, 1690.
v. Richard, b. 9 November, 1690; m. 16 March, 1715, Mary Silver, by whom he had several children; d. in 1771.
vi. Stephen, b. 12 April, 1693; m. 15 October, 1718, Sarah Swett; d. about 1744.
vii. Sarah, b. 3 February, 1695; m. 19 July, 1720, John Weed.
viii. Samuel, b. 21 March, 1697; d. in 1722.
ix. Benjamin, b. 24 March, 1699; m. 26 December, 1729, Judith Swett, by whom he had several children; d. 29 July, 1770.
{ Anne, b. 3 January, 1701; d. 6 January, 1701.
{ Mary, b. 3 January, 1701; d. 6 January, 1701.
xii. Margaret, b. 8 January, 1702.
xiii. Ann, b. 24 October, 1703; d. young.
xiv. Mary, b. 28 December, 1704; m. 13 November, 1728, Henry Dole of Newbury.
xv. Ruth, b. 17 November, 1706; m. 12 December, 1727, John Pearson of Rowley.
xvi. Anne, b. 18 January, 1710; m. 11 December, 1733, Daniel Knight of Newbury.

5. V.   John Hale, eldest son of John, born at Newbury 24 June, 1686; married 25 July, 1716, Patience, daughter of William Dole; she died 30 March, 1719, and he married secondly Mary ———; died in 1770. His will is printed page 42.   Children, born at Newbury:

i. Abigail, b. 1 August, 1717; d. 19 August, 1717.

ii. Patience, b. 22 March, 1719.   6

iii. Mehitable, b. in 1734; m. 28 January, 1752, Daniel Clarke; d. at Boscawen, N. H., 2 January, 1815.

iv. John, b. in 1736; m. 25 March, 1778, Mary Willett, by whom he had one daughter; d. 17 August, 1815; she d. 14 October, 1823.

v. Elizabeth, b. 1 March, 1741; m. 30 March, 1758, Stephen Swett.

vi. Nathaniel, b. 21 October, 1743.

6. VI. PATIENCE HALE, eldest child of John, born at Newbury 22 March, 1719; married at Newbury 1 March, 1739, Nathaniel Coffin of Falmouth; died at Falmouth 31 January, 1772; he died 12 January, 1766.

THE LOWLE FAMILY.

This family is traced back in England for several generations. The following pedigree is found at the British Museum in Ms. Harleian, 1559:

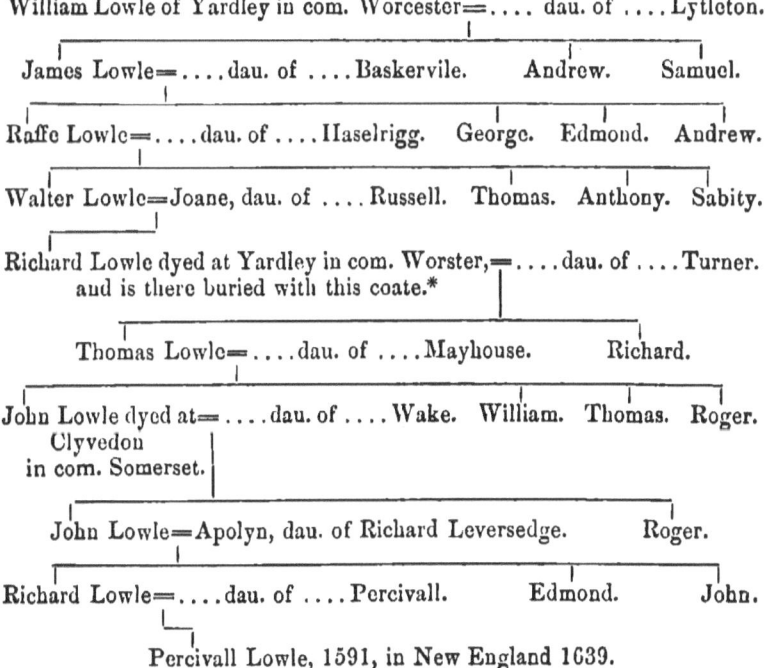

William Lowle of Yardley in com. Worcester=.... dau. of .... Lytleton.

James Lowle=....dau. of ....Baskervile.   Andrew.   Samuel.

Raffe Lowle=....dau. of ....Haselrigg.   George.   Edmond.   Andrew.

Walter Lowle=Joane, dau. of ....Russell.   Thomas.   Anthony.   Sabity.

Richard Lowle dyed at Yardley in com. Worster,=....dau. of ....Turner. and is there buried with this coate.*

Thomas Lowle=....dau. of ....Mayhouse.   Richard.

John Lowle dyed at=....dau. of ....Wake.   William.   Thomas.   Roger. Clyvedon in com. Somerset.

John Lowle=Apolyn, dau. of Richard Leversedge.   Roger.

Richard Lowle=....dau. of ....Percivall.   Edmond.   John.

Percivall Lowle, 1591, in New England 1639.

John Lowle of the eighth generation was of Portbury in Somersetshire, where he died in 1552, leaving a wife Apolyn, a son Richard, and a sister Mary Collins. Richard of the ninth generation lived at

---

* The Lowles bore, Sable, a dexter hand couped at the wrist, grasping three darts, one in pale and two in saltire, Argent.

Portbury; his wife was undoubtedly daughter of Edmund Percival* of Weston-in-Gordano, a neighboring parish, who belonged to the great family, from which descends the Earl of Egmont. Her ancestry may be read in various English works. Unfortunately the early parish registers of Clevedon, of Weston-in-Gordano, of Portbury, and of Kingston-Seymour, have all disappeared, leaving in doubt many facts, which their existence might prove, and forcing us to depend too much on uncertain conjectures.

X. PERCIVAL LOWLE, son of Richard, was of Kingston-Seymour and Portbury, Somersetshire, England; came to New England in 1639, and settled at Newbury; had wife Rebecca; he died 8 January, 1665; she died 28 December, 1645. Children, born in England:

    i. Richard, b. about 1602.   2
    ii. John, b. ———; was apprenticed in 1619 to Richard Baugh of Bristol, glover, and admitted citizen of Bristol in 1629; m. Mary ———, by whom he had several children; she d., and he m. secondly Elizabeth, daughter of widow Elizabeth Goodale of Newbury, by whom he had children; Freeman 2 June, 1641, Deputy 7 March, 1644; d. 10 July, 1647; she d. 23 April, 1651.
    iii. Joanna, b. ———; m. John Oliver of Newbury, and had an only child Mary;† he died in 1642, and she married secondly 17 April, 1645, William Gerrish of Newbury; d. 14 June, 1677; he d. at Salem 9 August, 1687.
    iv. Ann, b. ———; m. Thomas Milward of Newbury; he d. 1 September, 1653, and she m. secondly 26 December, 1654, Daniel Pierce of Newbury; d. 27 November, 1690; he d. 27 November, 1677.

2. XI. RICHARD LOWLE, probably elder son of Percival, born in England about 1602; came to New England with his father, bringing a wife, who died at Newbury in 1642; he married secondly Margaret ———; was a signer of the petition of 1666; he died 5 August, 1682, aged about 80. His will is printed page 6. Children:

    i. Percival, b. about 1639; m. at Newbury 7 September, 1664, Mary Chandler, by whom he had several children; she d. 5 February, 1708.
    ii. Rebecca, b. at Newbury 27 January, 1641.   3
    iii. Samuel, b. in Newbury in 1644; is said to have gone to England, and remained there.
    iv. Thomas, b. at Newbury 28 September, 1649; probably d. unmarried.

3. XII. REBECCA LOWLE, only daughter of Richard, born at Newbury 27 January, 1641; married 5 December, 1660, John Hale; died 1 June, 1662; he died 2 June, 1707.

* This Edmund Percival had four daughters, who in the "History of the House of Yvery" are said to have died without issue, but the manuscript there quoted as authority contains no such statement.
† Mary Oliver married Samuel Appleton of Ipswich, and was great-great-great-grandmother of the author.

THE JAQUES FAMILY.

HENRY JAQUES, first of the name in this country, was born in England, possibly in Wiltshire, about 1618; came to New England in 1640, and settled at Newbury; married 8 October, 1648, Ann, daughter of Richard Knight; was Freeman of the Colony of Massachusetts 19 May, 1669; was a carpenter, and employed in 1661 in building the new meeting-house at Newbury; in 1667 was an associate of Daniel Pierce in the grant of Woodbridge, New Jersey; died at Newbury 24 February, 1687, aged 69; she died 22 February, 1704. His will is printed page 15. Children, born at Newbury:

  i. Henry, b. 30 July, 1649; m. ———; moved to Woodbridge, N. J.; d. there before his father, leaving three sons.
  ii. Mary, b. 12 November, 1651; d. 13 October, 1653.
  iii. Mary, b. 23 October, 1653; m. 7 May, 1674, Richard Brown of Newbury; he d. 12 October, 1716.
  iv. Hannah, b. ———; m. 15 January, 1680, Ephraim Plummer of Newbury; he d. in ? 1715.
  v. Richard, b. in 1658; m. 18 January, 1682, Ruth, daughter of Samuel Plummer of Newbury, by whom he had a posthumous son Richard; d. 28 May, 1683.
  vi. Stephen, b. 9 September, 1661; m. 13 May, 1684. Deborah, daughter of Samuel Plummer of Newbury, by whom he had several children; d. in 1744.
  vii. Sarah, b. 20 March, 1664.   2
  viii. Daniel, b. 20 February, 1667; m. 20 March, 1693, Mary Williams of Newbury, by whom he had children; she d., and he m. secondly Susanna ———.
  ix. Elizabeth, b. 28 October, 1669; m. Richard Knight of Newbury.
  x. Ruth, b. 14 April, 1672; m. 29 November, 1692, Stephen Emery of Newbury; d. 9 January, 1764; he d. 1 February, 1747.
  xi. Abigail, b. 11 March, 1674; m. Benjamin Knight of Newbury; he d. in 1737.

2. II. SARAH JAQUES, fourth daughter of Henry, born at Newbury 20 March, 1664; married 10 October, 1683, John Hale, who died 4 March, 1726.

THE DOLE FAMILY.*

The researches of the late Horatio G. Somerby traced this family back to RICHARD DOLE of Rangeworthy, Gloucestershire, England, tanner. In his will, written 9 April, 1606, proved 12 September, 1609, he mentioned his wife Dorothy, his sons William and Giles, and his daughter Alice. From the register of the parish of Rangeworthy we learn that Richard Dole was buried there 29 May, 1609, and his son Giles 6 February, 1622; Alice married 1 June, 1614, Robert Hobbes.

* See New-England Historical and Genealogical Register, XXXVIII, 74.

2. II. WILLIAM DOLE, son of Richard, married at Rangeworthy 9 May, 1622, Joane Hale. Children, born at Rangeworthy:

 i. Richard, bapt. 31 December, 1622.   3
 ii. Dorothy, bapt. 11 April, 1624.
 iii. William, bapt. 5 February, 1626.
 iv. Joan, bapt. 28 December, 1628.

3. III. RICHARD DOLE, elder son of William, born at Rangeworthy in 1622; was called of Thornbury, a neighboring parish, when he apprenticed himself for seven years from 7 September, 1637, to John Lowle, then of Bristol, glover; came to New England with the Lowles in 1639, and settled at Newbury; married 3 May, 1647, Hannah, daughter of Henry Rolfe; was Deputy to the special General Court of 16 September, 1673, but apparently to no other; his wife died 16 November, 1678, and he married secondly 4 March, 1679, Hannah, widow of Samuel Brocklebank of Rowley; she died 6 September, 1690, and he married thirdly (the marriage-contract dated 29 October, 1690) Patience, probably daughter of Joseph Jewett of Rowley, widow of Shubael Walker; died in 1705. His will is printed page 18. Children, born at Newbury:

 i. John, b. 10 August, 1648; a Doctor; m. 23 October, 1676, Mary, daughter of William Gerrish of Newbury, by whom he had several children; d. in January, 1695.
 ii. Richard, b. 6 September, 1650; m. 7 June, 1677, Sarah, daughter of Stephen Greenleaf of Newbury, by whom he had several children; d. 1 August, 1723; she d. 1 September, 1718.
 iii. Ann, b. 26 March, 1652; d. 6 July, 1653.
 iv. Benjamin, b. 14 June, 1654; probably d. young.
 v. Joseph, b. 5 August, 1657; probably d. young.
 vi. William, b. 11 April, 1660.   4
 vii. Henry, b. 9 March, 1663; m. 3 November, 1686, Sarah, daughter of Samuel Brocklebank of Rowley, by whom he had two daughters; d. 13 September, 1690; she m. secondly 29 March, 1693, Nathaniel Coffin, and d. 20 April, 1750.
 viii. Hannah, b. 23 October, 1665; m. 18 May, 1692, John Moody of Newbury; he d. in ? 1737.
 ix. Apphia, b. 7 December, 1668; m. Peter Coffin of Gloucester; d. at Newbury 14 April, 1725; he d. 19 January, 1747.
 x. Abner, b. 8 March, 1672; m. 1 November, 1694, Mary, daughter of Jeremiah Jewett of Rowley, by whom he had a son; she d. 25 November, 1695, and he m. secondly at Boston 5 January, 1699, Sarah Belcher of Boston, by whom he had children; d. in 1739; she d. 21 July, 1730.

4. IV. WILLIAM DOLE, fifth son of Richard, born at Newbury 11 April, 1660; married 13 October, 1684, Mary, daughter of Samuel Brocklebank of Rowley; 31 March, 1685, William Dole and Mary Brocklebank, now his wife, owned to Ipswich Court the sin of fornication, and he was fined four pounds with fees, all of which was paid; he died 31 January, 1718. His will is printed page 34. Children, born at Newbury:

i. William, b. 12 January, 1685; m. 2 February, 1714, Rebecca, daughter of John Pearson of Rowley, by whom he had several children; d. 5 August, 1752.

ii. Hannah, b. 28 March, 1686; m. Richard Kelly.

iii. Mary, b. 1 February, 1688; m. in 1708 Joshua Boynton; d. 26 December, 1777; he d. 29 October, 1770.

iv. Richard, b. 31 December, 1689; m. 21 May, 1719, Sarah, daughter of Stephen Emery, by whom he had several children; d. 10 March, 1778.

v. Jane, b. 23 January, 1692; m. 17 August, 1711, Joseph Noyes.

vi. Patience, b. 8 April, 1694.   5

vii. Apphia, b. 13 May, 1696; d. 1 April, 1753.

viii. Samuel, b. 1 June, 1699; m. 30 October, 1720, Elizabeth Knight, by whom he had several children; d. 15 December, 1776.

ix. Benjamin, b. 2 July, 1702; m. ———— ———— ————————, by whom he had several children; d. 4 January, 1776.

5. V. PATIENCE DOLE, fourth daughter of William, born at Newbury 8 April, 1694; married 25 July, 1716, John Hale; died 30 March, 1719; he died in 1770.

THE ROLFE FAMILY.*

Much more of error than of fact has been printed about this family, which was founded in this country by two brothers John Rolfe and Henry Rolfe.

John Roaff, (so spelled), aged 50, with wife Ann and daughter Hester, of Melchitt Park, Wiltshire, England, came to New England from Southampton 24 April, 1638, in the Confidence of London; he was first of Newbury, Freeman 6 September, 1639, later of Salisbury; was a proprietor of Nantucket; died 8 February, 1664.

HENRY ROLFE was an early settler at Newbury; had wife Honour; died at Newbury 1 March, 1643; she died at Charlestown 19 December, 1650. His will is printed page 7; hers page 8. Children:

i. Ann, b. about 1626; m. Thomas Blanchard of Charlestown; he d. in 1651, and she m. secondly Richard Gardner of Charlestown and Woburn; he d. 29 May, 1698.

ii. Hannah, b. ————.   2

iii. John, b. ————; m. at Newbury 4 December, 1656, Mary, daughter of Samuel Scullard, by whom he had several children; lived at Newbury, Nantucket, and Cambridge; d. at Newbury 30 September, 1681.

iv. Benjamin, b. about 1638; m. at Newbury 3 November, 1659, Apphia, daughter of Thomas Hale, by whom he had several children; d. 10 August, 1710; she d. 24 December, 1708.

2. II. HANNAH ROLFE, daughter of Henry, born in England; married at Newbury 3 May, 1647, Richard Dole; died 16 November, 1678; he died 30 July, 1705.

* See New-England Historical and Genealogical Register, III., 149, XXXVI, 143.

The Foster Family.*

WILLIAM FOSTER, first of this family in New England, is found at Charlestown in 1652, in which year he and Ann his wife were admitted to the Church. Before this, all concerning him is conjecture. He was very possibly of Boston 1645 with a wife Susanna; he may also have been the passenger of his name in the Hercules from Southampton, England, in April, 1634; and this passenger was not improbably son of Richard Foster of Romsey in Hampshire, baptized there 22 January, 1615. At any rate

WILLIAM FOSTER of Charlestown married Ann, daughter of William Brackenbury; he was a sea-captain, and in 1669 master of the Dolphin; Cotton Mather in the "*Magnalia Christi Americana*," III. 183, has the following mention of him in the life of the Rev. John Eliot:

"There was a Godly Gentleman of *Charlstown*, one Mr. *Foster*, who with his Son, was taken Captive by *Turkish* Enemies. Much Prayer was employed, both privately and publickly, by the good People here, for the Redemption of that Gentleman; but we were at last informed, that the Bloody Prince, in whose Dominions he was now a Slave, was resolved that in his Life-time no Prisoner should be relased; and so the Distressed Friends of this Prisoner now concluded, *Our Hope is lost!* Well, upon this, Mr. *Eliot*, in some of his next Prayers, before a very solemn Congregation, very broadly beg'd, *Heavenly Father, work for the Redemption of thy poor Servant Foster; and if the Prince which detains him will not, as they say, dismiss him as long himself lives, Lord, we pray thee to kill that Cruel Prince; kill him, and glorify thy self upon him.* And now behold the Answer: The poor Captiv'd Gentleman quickly returns to us that had been mourning for him as a lost Man, and brings us News, that the Prince which had hitherto held him, was come to an *Untimely Death*, by which means he was now set at Liberty."

The dates of his captivity and release are approximately fixed. John Hull wrote in his diary 1671 "8 ber 21. We received intelligence that William Foster, master of a small ship, was taken by the Turks as he was going to Bilboa with fish. (He was redeemed, and came home 9ber 1673.)" Rev. Samuel Danforth of Roxbury wrote, "21. 8ᵐ. 1671 We heard yᵉ sad & heavy Tiding concerning yᵉ captivity of Capt. Foster & his sonn at Sally." "1673. 3ᵐ. Tidings concerning the redemption of mʳ Foster of Charlstown frō captivity after neer 18 moneth slavery and his return to London, his soun William coming home to his mother at Charlestown, having been his father's companion in bondage." "1673. 1. 10ᵐ. Captain Foster returned home after his Captivity." In the "AMERICAN HISTORICAL RECORD" for September, 1872, was printed a poem written by the

* See New England Historical and Genealogical Register, XXV, 67.

Rev. Michael Wigglesworth "Upon y⁰ return of my dear friend Mᵣ Foster wᵗʰ his son out of captivity under y⁰ Moors." 28 April, 1695, he was chosen Deacon of the Church of Charlestown, but "excused himself because of y⁰ Infirmity of his Age." His good social position is shown by the fact that his son Isaac stood first in rank in a class of eleven at Harvard College. He died 8 May, 1698, called on town-record "Navegatᵣ aged about 80 years "; she died 22 September, 1714. His will is printed page 36. Children, born at Charlestown:

i. William, b.——; only known as taken prisoner with his father.
ii. Isaac, b. in 1652; Harvard College 1671, Rev.; Fellow of Harvard College 22 May, 1678; Freeman of Massachusetts 2 October, 1678; in 1680 was settled over the First Church of Hartford, Conn.; m. the same year Mehitable, daughter of Samuel Wyllis of Hartford, widow of Daniel Russell of Charlestown, by whom he had a daughter Ann;* d. 20 August, 1682; she m. thirdly Rev. Timothy Woodbridge, his successor in the church of Hartford; d. 21 December, 1698.
iii. Sarah, b. in 1654; m. Benjamin Moore of Charlestown; he d. in 1680, and she m. secondly 9 August, 1682, Zechariah Long of Charlestown; he d. 28 March, 1688, and she m. thirdly 24 September, 1690, Caleb Stanly of Hartford, Conn.; d. 30 August, 1698.
iv. John, b. 15 July, 1656; d. 19 December, 1659.
v. Ann, b. in 1658; m. Eleazer Phillips of Charlestown; d. 1 December, 1695; he d. 29 April, 1709.
vi. Mary, b. in 1660; m. 8 August, 1676, James Smith of Charlestown; he d. 18 September, 1678, and she m. secondly 18 April, 1681, Timothy Phillips of Charlestown; d. 30 April, 1755; he d. 7 May, 1712.
vii. Richard, b. 10 August, 1663. 2
viii. Elizabeth, b. 5 April, 1665; m. 5 July, 1692, Isaac Goose or Vergoose, of Boston; d.? in 1757; he d. 29 November, 1710.
ix. John, b. 10 August, 1666; m. at Charlestown 31 May, 1692, Sarah Richardson of Newbury, by whom he had four daughters;† she d., and he m. secondly at Boston 22 September, 1718, Esther Lothrop; was a sea-captain; d. 14 June, 1723; she m. secondly 12 September, 1726, Francis Norwood of Gloucester.
x. Deborah, b. 28 February, 1668; d. 22 April, 1668.

2. II. RICHARD FOSTER, fourth son of William, born at Charlestown 10 August, 1663; married 4 May, 1686, Parnel, daughter and

* She m. 29 November, 1699, Rev. Thomas Buckingham of Hartford, who d. 19 November, 1731, and she m. secondly Rev. William Burnham of Kensington, Conn.; d. in 1765: he d. 23 September, 1750.
† The daughters were:
  i. Abigail, b. at Charlestown, 20 April, 1693; m. 11 May, 1710, Jabez Salter of Boston; he d. and she m. secondly 15 December, 1715, Edward Cruft of Boston.
  ii. Sarah, b. at Charlestown 31 August, 1696; d. 15 March, 1698.
  iii. Mary, b. at Boston 15 August, 1698; m. 26 June, 1717, Robert Nowell of Boston; he d., and she m. secondly 15 January, 1732, Samuel White of Boston.
  iv. Elizabeth, b. about 1713; m. 13 November, 1735, John Smart of Boston; he d., and she m. secondly 14 February, 1740, Sendall Williams of Boston.

heiress of Isaac Winslow; was a sea-captain; died in 1745; she died in 1751. His will is printed page 43. Children, born at Charlestown:

    i. Parnel, b. 23 February, 1687; d. 14 November, 1687.

    ii. Richard, b. 28 November, 1689; d. 11 February, 1694.

    iii. Mary, b. 16 February, 1692; m. 9 December, 1712, Samuel Cary of Charlestown; d. 23 December, 1718; he d. 27 February, 1741.

    iv. Richard, b. 23 March, 1694; m. Sarah, daughter of John Emerson of Charlestown, by whom he had four children;* she d. 16 November, 1724, and he m. secondly 21 October, 1725, Mary, daughter of John Foye of Charlestown, by whom he had eleven children;* was High-Sheriff of Middlesex, 1731–64, Associate Justice of Court of Common Pleas for Middlesex, 1764–71; d. 29 August, 1774;† she d. 26 October, 1774.

    v. Parnel, b. 25 August, 1696; m. in 1718 John Codman of Charlestown; d. 15 September, 1752; he d. in 1755.

    vi. Ann, b. 8 November, 1699; m. 6 November, 1721, Rev. Daniel Perkins of Bridgewater; d. 7 July, 1750; he d. 29 September, 1782.

    vii. Sarah, b. 16 November, 1701; m. 19 July, 1723, Dr. Peter Calef of Charlestown, who d. 11 October, 1735.

    viii. Isaac, b. 3 January, 1704.   3

    ix. Elizabeth, b. 21 August, 1706; m. Timothy McDaniel of Charlestown; d. 22 October, 1766; he d. 10 November, 1766.

    x. Katharine, b. 6 April, 1713; d. 11 February, 1716.

3. III. ISAAC FOSTER, youngest son of Richard, born at Charlestown 3 January, 1704; married 24 August, 1732, Eleanor, daughter of William Wyer; was a sea-captain, making frequent voyages between Boston and Europe, and afterwards a merchant; was a prominent citizen of Charlestown, taking an active part in public affairs during the years just before the Revolution, and his name often occurs in the History of the Town; after the burning of Charlestown he lived at Boston, where he died 27 December, 1780; she died at Charlestown 5 March, 1798. Children, born at Charlestown:

    i. William, b. 27 May, 1733; Harvard College 1752; d. 3 December, 1759.

---

* Of these fifteen children, two died in infancy, five others certainly died unmarried; the other eight were all daughters and born at Charlestown, viz.:—

    i. Sarah, b. in 1718; m. 22 March, 1738, Samuel Bradstreet of Charlestown; d. in 1802; he d. in 1755.

    ii. Mary, b. in 1722; m. 18 June, 1741, John Breed of Charlestown, who d. in 1755, and she m. secondly 25 April, 1765, John White of Charlestown; d. in 1814.

    iii. Elizabeth, b. 17 September, 1726; m. 9 December, 1748, David Cheever.

    iv. Parnel, b. 24 August, 1729; m. 13 October, 1763, Richard Boylston of Charlestown; d. 28 July, 1796; he d. 30 June, 1807.

    v. Hannah, b. in 1731; m. 22 November, 1753, Ebenezer Kent of Charlestown; d. soon; he d. in 1767.

    vi. Ann, b. 24 July, 1736; m. 29 October, 1767, John Austin of Charlestown; d. 27 January, 1798; he d. 16 October, 1824.

    vii. Katharine, b. in 1738; m. in 1772, John Sprague of Lancaster, C. J. C. C. P. for Worcester; d. at Lancaster 5 May 1787; he d. 28 September, 1800.

    viii. Abigail, b. in 1739 or 1740; m. 22 September, 1768, Isaac Codman.

† An engraving of his tomb, with a Foster coat of arms, may be seen in the HERALDIC JOURNAL for 1865.

ii. Isaac, b. in 1738; d. young.
iii. Isaac, b. 28 August, 1740; Harvard College 1758; m. 4 July, 1765, Martha, daughter of Thaddeus Mason of Cambridge, by whom he had three daughters;* she died 21 September, 1770, and he m. secondly, 8 September, 1771, Mary, daughter of Richard Russell of Charlestown, by whom he had two daughters;* was a physician, and a prominent citizen; member of the first Provincial Congress of Massachusetts in October, 1774; surgeon in the service of the United Colonies, 1775–80; d. at Boston 27 February, 1781;† she m. secondly, 8 June, 1783, John Hurd of Boston, and d. 14 January, 1786.
iv. Thomas, b. in 1741; d. young.
v. Edward, b. in 1744; d. young.
vi. Eleanor, b. 4 August, 1746.   4
vii. Richard, b. in 1748; d. young.

4. IV. Eleanor Foster, only daughter of Isaac, born at Charlestown, 4 August, 1746; married at Charlestown 30 October, 1769, Dr. Nathaniel Coffin of Portland; died at Portland 8 September, 1822; he died 18 October, 1826.

The following notice appeared in the Continental Journal of Thursday, 4 January, 1781:

On Wednesday evening the 27th ult. died at his House in Back Street, of a paralitic disorder, Capt. Isaac Foster, aged 78, late of the unfortunate town of Charlestown. This Gentleman early in life entered into the Sea service, in which his diligence, activity and fidelity, soon raised him to a considerable command, after having made near forty voyages to Europe, as commander of a vessel, he returned to his family to remain with them, and promised himself in his old age, a rich enjoyment with his friends and family, of the labours of his youth; in this wish he was in a great measure indulged, and was honored with the principal offices of the town he resided in, until the commencement of hostilities between Great-Britain and America; upon which he took an open and active part in the cause of his country, by the destruction of Charlestown, at the memorable battle of Bunker-Hill, he was striped of great part of his hard earned property, and driven from his home. What was most distinguishing in his character, was a truly catholic disposition, which inclined him to think the best of all sects of christians, a benevolence of heart,

---

* The daughters were:
i. Martha, b. at Charlestown 11 May, 1766; d. 4 May, 1768.
ii. Eleanor, b. at Charlestown 4 November, 1767; m. 8 January, 1804, Thomas Bellows of Walpole, N. H.; d. 29 August, 1840; he d. 18 April, 1848.
iii. Martha, b. at Charlestown 19 September, 1769; d. young.
iv. Mary Beal, b. at Charlestown 17 August, 1774; m. in 1792 William Pratt of Boston, afterwards of Liverpool, England, where she d. 15 August, 1836; he d. 5 February, 1842.
v. Nancy or Ann, b. at Boston 9 October, 1777; m. at Walpole, N. H., 28 May, 1819, Edward Reynolds of Boston; d. 1 January, 1866; he d. 2 November, 1848.

† See in Atlantic Monthly for May, 1859, "A Bundle of Old Letters." With him seems to have ended the male line of descendants of William Foster.

7

that made him always ready to assist the distressed, a love to his country, which disposed him to make the greatest sacrifices in its service; but above all, an uncommon openness, honesty and integrity of mind, which alone, if there is any justice in Mr. Pope's remark, is no small character,

> "A Wit's a Feather, and a Chief's a Rod,
> An honest Man's the noblest work of God."

The Brackenbury Family.

WILLIAM BRACKENBURY, born in England about 1602, was among the early settlers of New England, coming probably in the fleet with Winthrop, 1630, with wife Ann and daughter Ann; lived at Charlestown; was one of those desiring to be made Freemen 19 October, 1630, but was not Freeman till 4 March, 1633; was Constable of Charlestown 1638, and Selectman; moved to Malden, where he was a prominent citizen; had a second wife Alice; died in August, 1668, aged 66; she died 28 December, 1670, or 24 January, 1671, aged 70. His will is printed page 23. Children:

 i. Ann, b. in England about 1629.   2
 ii. Mary, b. at Charlestown in 1634; m. John Ridgway of Malden; d. 24 December, 1670.
 iii. Samuel, b. at Charlestown 10 February, 1646; Harvard College 1664; Freeman 7 May, 1673; was a physician, but preached at Rowley two years, probably about 1669-71; m. Mercy, daughter of Rev. Michael Wigglesworth of Malden, by whom he had children;* lived at Malden, but moved to Boston, where he d. 16 January, 1678; she m. secondly Rev. Samuel Belcher of Ipswich, and d. 14 November, 1728.

2. II. ANN BRACKENBURY, eldest child of William, born in England about 1629; was undoubtedly the child of nine years, who figures in a painful adventure in the Addenda to Winthrop's History of New England under date of 1637. 5. 3; married William Foster; died 22 September, 1714, aged 85; he died 8 May, 1698.

The Winslow Family.†

This family is traced back with sufficient certainty to KENELM WINSLOW of Kempsey, Worcestershire, England, who is recorded as living in 1559, and several years before and after; he had two sons, Richard and Edward, and is probably the same person as Kenelm Winslow of St. Andrew's in the city of Worcester, who died

---

* See New-England Historical and Genealogical Register, XLVI., 178.
† See Thacher's History of Plymouth, Deane's History of Scituate, the New-England Historical and Genealogical Register, IV. 297, XVII. 159, XXI. 209, XXV. 355, XXVI. 69, and the Winslow Memorial.

in 1607, leaving wife Katherine, and children and grandchildren. Unfortunately for our positive information concerning the family, the early register of Kempsey is lost, the oldest volume dating only from 1688; the early register of St. Andrew's, Worcester, is also missing.

Richard Winslow, son of Kenelm, married Alice, daughter of Edward Hardman, lived at Kempsey, and died 20 May, 1659, leaving children.

2. II. EDWARD WINSLOW, son of Kenelm, married at St. Bride's, Fleet Street, London, 4 November, 1594, Magdalen Oliver; lived at Droitwich, Worcestershire; nothing is known of the date of his death, except that it was before 1631. Children, born at Droitwich:

    i. Edward, b. 18 October, 1595; joined the Pilgrims at Leyden in Holland in 1617; m. there 16 May, 1618, Elizabeth Barker; came to New England in the Mayflower, 1620; his wife d. at Plymouth 24 March, 1621, and he m. secondly, 12 May, 1621, Susanna, widow of William White; lived at Marshfield, was often an Assistant, and three years Governor of Plymouth Colony; d. on an expedition against the Spanish West Indies 8 May, 1654, leaving a son and daughter; she d. at Marshfield 1 October, 1680.

    ii. John, b. 17 April, 1597.   3

    iii. Elenor, b. 23 April, 1598.

    iv. Kenelm, b. 2 May, 1599; probably came to New England in 1629; m. in June, 1634, Elinor, widow of John Adams of Plymouth, by whom he had several children; lived at Marshfield; d. at Salem 12 September, 1672; she d. at Marshfield 5 December, 1681.

    v. Gilbert, b. 28 October, 1600; came in the Mayflower 1620; lived only a few years at Plymouth; returned to England, where he d. before 1650.

    vi. Elizabeth, b. 1 March, 1602; d. in 1605.

    vii. Magdalen, b. 26 December, 1604.

    viii. Josiah, b. 11 February, 1606; came to New England in 1631, landing at Saco; m. at Scituate, where he lived for a time, Margaret Bourne, by whom he had several children; settled at Marshfield, where he d. 1 December, 1674; she d. in 1683.

3. III. JOHN WINSLOW, second son of Edward, born at Droitwich 17 April, 1597; came to Plymouth in the Fortune, 1623; married about 1627 Mary, daughter of James Chilton; moved to Boston in 1657; was a signer of the petition of 1666; died in 1674; she died in 1679. His will is printed page 24, and hers page 27. Children, all probably born at Plymouth:

    i. Susannah, b. ———; m. in 1649 Robert Latham of Plymouth.

    ii. Mary, b. in 1630; m. 16 January, 1651, Edward Gray of Plymouth; d. in 1663; he d. in June, 1681.

    iii. John, b. ———; m. Elizabeth ———, by whom he had children; she d., and he m. secondly Judith ———; d. in October, 1683.

    iv. Edward, b. about 1634; m. Sarah, daughter of William Hilton, grand-daughter of Edmund Greenleaf (p. 55), by whom he had children; she d. 4 April, 1667, and he m. secondly Elizabeth, daughter of Edward Hutchinson, by whom he had children; d. in 1682.

v. Sarah, b. ———; m. at Boston 19 July, 1660, Miles Standish; he d. soon, and she m. secondly in November, 1666, Tobias Payne; he d. 12 September, 1669, and she m. thirdly, in 1672, Richard Middlecott; d. 10 June, 1726; he d. 13 June, 1704.

vi. Joseph, b. ———; m. Sarah, daughter of Thomas Lawrence, by whom he had children; moved to Long Island; d. in 1679; she m. secondly Charles Labros.

vii. Samuel, b. in 1641; m. Hannah, daughter of Walter Briggs of Boston, by whom he had children; d. 14 October, 1680.   4

viii. Isaac, b. about 1644.

ix. Benjamin, b. 12 August, 1653; d. before 1676.

4. IV. ISAAC WINSLOW, fifth son of John, born at Plymouth about 1644; married at Charlestown, 14 August, 1666, Mary, daughter of Increase Nowell; was a merchant; died at Port Royal, Jamaica, in August 1670; she married secondly 10 September, 1674, John Long of Charlestown; died in 1728. His will is printed page 38, and hers page 38. Children, born at Charlestown:

i. Parnel, b. 14 November, 1667.   5
ii. Isaac, b. 22 July, 1670; d. 24 or 25 August, 1670.

5. V. PARNEL WINSLOW, only surviving child of Isaac, born at Charlestown 14 November, 1667; married 4 May, 1686, Richard Foster; died in 1751; he died in 1745.

THE CHILTON FAMILY.

JAMES CHILTON came to Plymouth in the Mayflower in 1620 with his wife and daughter Mary. He died on board 8 December, 1620, and his wife died soon after. According to Gov. Bradford's record, "They had an other doughter, y^t was married, came afterward." The Rev. Henry M. Dexter found on the records of Leyden in Holland several entries of the name of Chilton in curious forms of Dutch spelling. One of these is the marriage 22 July, 1615, of Roger Chandler clothworker from Colchester and Isabella Tgiltron from Canterbury. This undoubtedly gives us the former residence of James Chilton, for Roger Chandler is found later at Plymouth, and was dead in 1665. Mr. Joseph M. Cowper of Canterbury, who has carefully studied the registers of the parish-churches of that city, and edited some of them for publication, has found the baptisms and burials of several children of a James Chilton between 1584 and 1599. Among them are the baptism of an Isabell at St. Paul's 15 January 1587, and the burial of a Mary at St. Martin's 23 November, 1593. Unfortunately he has not yet found the baptism of a second Mary, who might have come with her parents to New England, nor has he found the father and baptism of James the Pilgrim.

MARY CHILTON, daughter of James, the heroine of tradition as the first to leap on Plymouth rock, married about 1627 John Winslow; died at Boston in 1679; he died in 1674.

THE NOWELL FAMILY.

INCREASE NOWELL was one of the prominent among the early founders of Massachusetts. It has been often stated that "his father or grandfather was brother to the famous Alexander Nowell, Dean of St. Paul's in the reign of Queen Elizabeth," and therefore that he belonged to the very respectable family of Nowell of Read and Great Merlay, in the parish of Whalley, Lancashire, England. Researches made for me have as yet failed to prove this connection; but it has been found impossible to obtain any trace of certain nephews of Dean Alexander Nowell, sons of his brother Laurence, Dean of Lichfield. I presume one of them was father of Increase.

The first mention we have of Increase Nowell is a bequest in the will of John Hale of London, grocer, 10 August, 1620: "Item I give to Gilbert Marshall and Increse Nowell (yf they deliver up orderlie Accompts) the somme of tenne poundes apeece to be payed in five yeres after my decease." He was one of the grantees named in the Royal Charter of Massachusetts Bay, dated 4 March, 1629, and he appears as a very regular attendant at the meetings of the Government in England. He was one of the twelve men, who signed the agreement at Cambridge in August, 1629, pledging themselves to go to New England by March, 1630. He was then living at Wapping, London, with his wife Parnel,* daughter of Thomas Gray of Harwich in Essex, widow of ―――― Parker. He came to New England in the great fleet in 1630. He was a member of the First Church of Boston or Charlestown, at which latter town he remained when the Church was moved to Boston. He was the principal gentleman among those who stayed at Charlestown, being the only one dignified with the title Esq. He was an Assistant in the Government of Massachusetts by election every year from the first till his death, and acted as Secretary 1636–50. He was a Selectman of Charlestown nearly every year from 1635 till his death. He was chosen Ruling Elder of the First Church at its foundation, but in 1632 resigned this position, which was thought not compatible with his civil office. Roger Williams wrote to Gov. Winthrop, "You lately sent musick to our eares, when we heard you perswaded (& that effectually & successfully) our beloved Mr. Nowell to surrender up one sword."

* See New England Historical and Genealogical Register, XXXIV, 253.

In 1634 the General Court granted him two hundred acres of land on the west side of the North River, otherwise called the Three Mile Brook. In 1635 he was fined iij^s iiij^d for selling wine, but a note in the margin of the records states that "it was lefte in trust wth him by a friend, to sell for him." In 1636 he was one of the Magistrates to keep particular Courts for Newe Towne, Waterton, Charlton, Meadford and Concord. In 1639 the General Court granted him 500 acres of land on the north side of the bounds of Concord. He was often appointed by the General Court to serve on important committees, and in 1645 was one of the Committee for the County of Middlesex "to consid^r of & drawe up a body of lawes, & p^{r}sent y^m to ye consid^{r}ation of ye next Gen^{r}all Co^{r}t." In 1653, the Court, taking heed of the poor condition of the College, appointed a Committee, of which Increase Nowell was chairman, "to examine the state of the colledge in all respects," especially in several particular points, with full authority to act in all the premises.

Increase Nowell died 1 November, 1655, and the same month the General Court passed the following vote:—"Itt is desired, that the depu^{ts} of each toune co$\bar{m}$end the condi$\bar{c}$on of Mr Nowells family to theire severall tounes, in referenc to some meete recompence for the said Mr Nowells service, by way of rate or otherwise, bringing theire retournes to the next Court of Election." In October, 1656, " The Court, being sencible of the lowe condi$\bar{c}$on of the late honnored Mr Nowells family, & remembring his long service to this co$\bar{m}$onwealth, in the place not only of a magistrate, but secretary also, for wch he had but litle and slender recompenc, & the countries debts being such as out of the country rate they cannot comfortably make such an honnorable recompenc to his family as otherwise they would, judge meete therefore, do give & graunt to Mrs Nowell and hir sonne Samuell two thowsand acres of land, to be laid out by Mr Thomas Danforth and Robert Hale, in any part of the countrie not yett graunted to others, in two or three farmes, that may not hinder any planta$\bar{c}$on to be errected." In April, 1657, the two thousand acres were laid out on Cocheco river beyond the bounds of Dover. 6 May, 1657, the Court also ordered Messrs. Danforth and Hale to lay out for Mr. Nowell's executors the three thousand two hundred acres of land granted in 1650 to Nowell and Thomas Dudley, as executors of the will of Isaac Johnson, which land was in 1664 laid out in Marlborough bounds near Quansigamug Pond.

Edward Johnson, in his "Wonder-working Providence of Sions Saviour in New England," 1654, wrote thus of Increase Nowell:—

"Increase shalt thou, with honour now, in this thy undertaking,
    Thou hast remain'd as yet unstaind, all errors foule forsaking;
To poore and rich, thy Justice much hath manifested bin:
    Like Samuel Nathanaell, Christ hath thee fram'd within;
Thy faithfulnesse, people expresse, and Secretary they

Chose thee each year, by which appeare, their love with thee
doth stay.

Now Nowell see Christ call'd hath thee, and work thou must for him,
  In beating down the triple Crown, and all that his foes ben.

Thus doest thou stand by Christ fraile man, to tell his might can make
  Dust do his will, with graces fill, till dust to him he take."

The Rev. William I. Budington spoke thus of Increase Nowell in
his lectures on the History of the First Church, Charlestown : —
" He more than any other man, may be considered the father of the
church and the town. He was a zealous Puritan, an active and
devout Christian, and deserves to be held in grateful esteem by the
citizens of this Commonwealth, and especially by the inhabitants of
this town."

Parnell Nowell, his widow, died at Charlestown, 25 March, 1687,
aged 84. His will is printed page 29. Children :

  i. Joseph, b. at Wapping, London, in 1629 ; d. in 1629.
  ii. Increase, b. at Charlestown 19 November, 1630 ; d. 6 March, 1632.
  iii. Abigail, b. at Charlestown 27 April, 1632 ; d. 6 March, 1634.
  iv. Samuel, b. at Charlestown 12 November, 1634 ; Harvard College
      1653, Rev.; Fellow of Harvard 28 February, 1655 ; studied for
      the ministry, but was never settled; chaplain to the army in the
      Narragansett campaign 1675, and at other times; in 1678
      preached the Artillery-Election sermon, which was printed;
      Freeman of the Colony of Massachusetts 23 May, 1677 ; an As-
      sistant 1680-6, a Commissioner of the United Colonies 1684-6,
      Treasurer of the Colony of Massachusetts 1685-6 ; m. Mary,
      daughter of William Alford of Boston, widow first of Peter But-
      ler of Boston, secondly of Hezekiah Usher of Cambridge, had no
      children ; d. in London in September, 1688, being there on
      behalf of the Colony ; she d. at Boston 4 August, 1693.
  v. Eliezer, b. at Charlestown 16 November, 1636; d. 26 November,
      1636.
  vi. Mehitable, b. at Charlestown 2 February, 1638; m. 16 September,
      1659, William Hilton of Charlestown ; he d. 7 September, 1675,
      and she m. secondly 29 October, 1684, John Cutler of Charles-
      town ; d. 29 September, 1711; he d. 12 September, 1694.
  vii. Increase, b. at Charlestown in 1640 ; a sailor, of whom no more is
      known.
  viii. Mary, b. at Charlestown 26 May, 1643.   2
  ix. Alexander, b. at Charlestown in 1645 ; Harvard College 1664;
      Fellow of Harvard 28 November, 1666 ; Freeman 31 May,
      1671 ; was author of several almanacs ; d. 13 July, 1672, " after
      long sicknesse and furious distraction and madnesse," according
      to the Rev. Samuel Danforth.

2. II. MARY NOWELL, youngest daughter of Increase, born at
Charlestown 26 May, 1643 ; married 14 August, 1666, Isaac
Winslow ; he died in August, 1670, and she married secondly 10
September, 1674, John Long of Charlestown, and had children ; she
died in 1728 ; he died 20 July, 1683.

THE WYER FAMILY.*

EDWARD WYER, a Scotchman, born about 1622, is first found in New England at Charlestown in 1658; he married 5 January, 1659, Elizabeth, daughter of William Johnson; died 3 May, 1693, aged 71, called on town record "an aged Scotsman"; she married secondly before 1697 William Munroe of Cambridge and Lexington; died 14 December, 1715. His will is printed page 40. Children, born at Charlestown:

  i. Elizabeth, b. 10 November, 1659; m. Benjamin Mirick of Charlestown.
 ii. Edward, b. ———; m. 1 September, 1684, Abigail, daughter of John Lawrence of Charlestown; d. soon, and she m. secondly 25 December, 1689, Nicholas Lawrence of Charlestown; he d. 28 February, 1711, and she m. thirdly Edward Clifford; d. 11 February, 1727.
iii. Robert, b. 10 February, 1664; m. 26 June, 1688, Elizabeth, daughter of John Fowle of Charlestown; she d. 20 January, 1690, and he m. secondly Ruth, daughter of John Johnson of Haverhill, by whom he had several children; d. 14 November, 1709; she d. 26 December, 1742.
 iv. Hannah, b. in 1665; m. 15 December, 1686, Nathan Dunkin or Dunklin of Charlestown.
  v. Katharine, b. 5 December, 1666; m. Jonathan Welch of Charlestown; d. 4 February, 1709.
 vi. Nathaniel, b. 14 June, 1668; probably d. young.
vii. Ruhamah, b. 24 December, 1670; m. in 1696 John Hill of Boston.
viii. Eliezer, b. 12 December, 1672; m. Catharine, daughter of Jonathan Wade of Medford, by whom he had several children; lived at Medford, perhaps moved to Dover, N. H.
 ix. Zachariah, b. 16 March, 1676; m. at Concord 7 June, 1698, Mary Jones, by whom he had children, born at Boston; lived at Boston; d. 23 November, 1717.
  x. Sarah, b. 5 March, 1678; m. John Fillebrown.
 xi. William, b. 3 October, 1680.   2

2. II. WILLIAM WYER, youngest child of Edward, born at Charlestown 3 October, 1680; married 26 October, 1701, Eleanor, daughter of Thomas Jenner; was a sea-captain; died in February, 1749; she died in December, 1747. His will is printed page 45. Children:

  i. William, b. at Boston 26 March, 1703; d. at Charlestown 7 February, 1710.
 ii. Thomas, b. at Charlestown 14 October, 1704; m. 12 November, 1724, Katharine, daughter of Jonathan Dowse of Charlestown, by whom he had children; d. before 1747; she m. secondly 12 May, 1747, Isaac Johnson of Charlestown; d. at Concord 8 November, 1782.

* See New England Historical and Genealogical Register, XXV, 246, XLVI, 178, and Wyman's Genealogies and Estates of Charlestown.

iii. Edward, b. at Charlestown 8 July, 1706 ; m. Elizabeth ———, by whom he had a daughter ; she d. 28 June, 1730, and he m. secondly ——— ———, and had Edward,* b. in 1751.

iv. William, b. at Charlestown 11 July, 1710 ; d. 17 December, 1721.

v. David, b. at Charlestown 24 February, 1712 ; m. 2 February, 1739, Rebecca, daughter of Daniel Russell of Charlestown, by whom he had several children ; moved to Falmouth, Me.†

vi. Eleanor, b. at Charlestown 14 July, 1714.   3

3. III. ELEANOR WYER, only daughter of William, born at Charlestown 14 July, 1714 ; married 24 August, 1732, Isaac Foster ; died 5 March, 1798 ; he died at Boston 27 December, 1780.

THE JOHNSON FAMILY.‡

WILLIAM JOHNSON with wife Elizabeth settled at Charlestown in 1634 ; was Freeman of the Colony of Massachusetts 4 March, 1635 ; was a brickmaker ; died 9 December, 1677 ; she married secondly 24 October, 1679, Thomas Carter of Charlestown ; died 6 October, 1684. His will is printed page 30. Children :

i. John, b. in 1633 ; m. at Charlestown 15 October, 1656, Elizabeth, daughter of Elias Maverick, by whom he had children ; she d. 22 March, 1674, and he m. secondly 3 March, 1675, widow Sarah Gillo of Lynn ; she d. 24 July, 1676, and he m. thirdly 8 September, 1680, Catharine, daughter of ——— Skipper, widow of John Maverick of Charlestown ; moved in 1658 to Haverhill, where he lived, and with his wife was killed by Indians 29 August, 1708.

ii. Ruhamah, b. at Charlestown in 1635 ; m. 25 April, 1654, John Knight of Charlestown ; probably d. in 1659 ; he d. 1 December, 1714.

iii. Joseph, b. at Charlestown in 1637 ; m. 19 April, 1664, Mary Soatlie of Charlestown ; she d. 22 March, 1665, and he m. secondly in 1666 Hannah, daughter of Thomas Tenny of Rowley, by whom he had children ; lived at Haverhill ; d. 18 November, 1714.

iv. Elizabeth, b. at Charlestown in 1639.   2

v. Jonathan, b. at Charlestown in 1641 ; m. at Marlborough 14 October, 1663, Mary Newton, by whom he had children ; soldier 1676 ; lived at Marlborough ; d. 21 April, 1712 ; she d. 28 December, 1728.

vi. Nathaniel, b. at Charlestown about 1643 ; m. 24 November, 1668, Joanna Long of Cambridge, by whom he had children ; d. about 1678 ; she m. secondly 10 December, 1678, Christopher Goodwin of Charlestown.

---

* This Edward m. Alice ——— ; was a physician ; of Halifax, N. S., 1785, afterwards of Cambridge ; d. at Menotomy 16 September, 1788, leaving Edward, William and Alice.
† See Sabine's American Loyalists.
‡ See New England Historical and Genealogical Register, XXXIII.

vii. Zachariah, b. at Charlestown in 1645; m. Elizabeth, daughter of
John Jefts of Boston, by whom he had children; soldier 1675–6;
moved to Boston, where he d. 25 December, 1727; she d. 8
April, 1717.

viii. Isaac, b. at Charlestown in 1649; m. 22 November, 1671, Mary,
daughter of Nicholas Stone of Boston, by whom he had children;
soldier 1675–6; d. at Charlestown 31 August, 1711; she d. in
1732.

2. II. ELIZABETH JOHNSON, younger daughter of William, born
at Charlestown in 1639; married 5 January, 1659, Edward Wyer;
he died 3 May, 1693, and she married secondly before 1697 William Munroe of Cambridge and Lexington; died 14 December,
1715; he died 27 January, 1718.

THE JENNER FAMILY.*

The publication by the Massachusetts Historical Society, Volume
XXXVII. 355, of letters of the Rev. THOMAS JENNER attracted my
attention to him, and it soon appeared that descendants from him
are living in this country. He was probably born in one of the
Eastern Counties of England, where he may also have been a settled
clergyman. The Rev. Robert Stansby, who wrote of Mr. Jenner in
1637 in a letter in the above-mentioned volume, may have meant
the emigrant, and have been ignorant of his departure from England.

He came to New England about 1635, and soon became the
minister of Weymouth, where eighteen acres of land were granted
to him in June, 1636; he was Freeman of the Colony of Massachusetts 8 December, 1636. From an expression of the Rev.
Stephen Bachiler, on page 104 of the volume quoted before, I judge
him to have been somewhat advanced in life at the time of his
coming. His ministry at Weymouth was unfortunate; Winthrop
and Hubbard mention the differences between the people and Mr.
Jenner. In the latter part of 1640 he moved to Saco, where he is
thought to have been the first settled minister. His arrival was
regarded with favor by Thomas Gorges and Richard Vines, and the
People "willingly contributed for his stipend 47 li. per annum."
He had, however, some "hot discourses, especially about the ceremonies," and 28 March, 1646, he wrote to Governor Winthrop,
"Mr. Vines is fallen out with me bitterly, and threatens me to my
face, when time shall serve." He thereupon resigned his ministry,
and soon left Saco.

We next hear of him in England in October, 1650, and April,
1651, as living in Norfolk,† and compelled by poverty to part with
his library, which was sold to the Corporation for the Propagation

* See New England Historical and Genealogical Register, XIX., 246.
† See Hutchinson's Collection of Original Papers, I. 257 & 260, and Hazard's State
Papers, II. 180 & 187.

of the Gospel in New England.* The name of his wife is unknown, and the date of his death; he had certainly three children, two daughters, who are known only from one of his letters, and a son Thomas.

2. II. THOMAS JENNER, junior, probably came to New England with his father, and received at the same time forty-five acres of land at Weymouth; was Freeman 6 September, 1639, and was, I doubt not, the Deputy to the General Court in 1640; in 1636 he was also admitted an inhabitant of Charlestown, where we find him in 1649. The following deed is found in the first volume at the Suffolk Registry, and in the first volume of "Estates" at the State House: —

"28 (10) 1649 Thomas Jenner of Charlestowne granted unto Elder Edw. Bates & John Whitman of Waymouth one dwelling house at Waymouth (now in possession of John King) two orchyards & twenty-one Acres adjoyning more or lesse, also twelve Acres at the westerne neck be it more or lesse, also half an Acre uppon Grape Iland be it more or lesse, also fourty Acres wch is his owne pp lott be it more or lesse, & eighteene Acres wch was his fathers. Also the round marsh being foure Acres more or lesse and one Acre of fresh marsh adjoyning, & six Acres of marsh above the fresh pond, & a wood lott on hingham side. And this was by an absolute deed of sale dated 28 (10) 1649, & consented to by m^{rs} Jenner before m^r Nowell."

I presume his wife was Esther Jenner, who joined the Church of Charlestown 9 July, 1648, but this may have been a sister. According to the diary of Samuel Sewall, she seems to have married secondly a Mr. Winsley, and to have been his widow in 1686. Thomas Jenner had certainly two children, John and Thomas; I do not know the date of his death or that of his wife.

John Jenner, undoubtedly son of Thomas of Charlestown, was of Stratford, Conn., before 1650, and was one of the original founders in 1655 of Brookhaven, Long Island, which was settled by emigrants mostly from the neighborhood of Boston; he is named in the patent of 7 May, 1666; he seems to have married Alice, daughter of Robert Pigg of New Haven, by whom he had Mary, b. in 1648, Thomas, b. in 1651, and probably John and Samuel† of Woodbury, Conn.; his son Thomas of Brookhaven m. at Charlestown, where his cousins lived, 9 July, 1685, Marah, daughter of Nicholas March, and had there Martha, b. 29 May, 1687, and Elizabeth, b. in 1689.

3. III. THOMAS JENNER, son of Thomas of Charlestown, born about 1630; married at Charlestown 22 May, 1655, Rebecca, daughter of Nicholas Trerice; was member of the Artillery Company of Boston 1673; was a sea-captain, and made regular trips

* The original catalogue of the library is in Ms. Rawlinson, C. 934, in the Bodleian Library at Oxford.

† For descendants of this Samuel see Cothren's History and Genealogy of Ancient Woodbury, and History of Pittsford, Vt.

botween England and New England; was a prisoner in Africa in 1680. IIe seems to have inherited a taste for the ministry; John Dunton, who came to Boston as his passenger in 1685, describes him thus: — " Our Captain, *Tho. Jenner*, was a rough Covetous *Tarpaulin ;* but he understood his Business well enough, and had *some smatt'rings of Divinity in his Head.* IIe went to Prayers very constantly, and took upon him to EXPOUND the Scriptures, which gave Offence to several of the Passengers." IIe died in England in the autumn of 1686; * in 1708 his heirs were the widow, son David, and daughters Rebecca Lewis, Elizabeth Bur, and Elenor Wyer; his widow desired "allowance for the Funerall Charges of the said deceased, paid in England, £18 is here £22.10;" she died at Charlestown 23 September, 1722, aged 86. Children, born at Charlestown :

i. Rebecca, b. 27 February, 1656; m. 3 June, 1673, Samuel Lynde of Charlestown; he d. in 1681, and she m. secondly, 6 April, 1682, Robert Lewis of Charlestown, who d. before 170S.
ii. Thomas, b. 20 September, 1658; a soldier in the Narragansett campaign; d. before 1688.
iii. David, b. 20 October, 1663; m. 14 June, 1688, Mabel, daughter of James Russell of Charlestown, by whom he had six children;† d. 23 or 24 August, 1709.
iv. Sarah, b. 17 July, 1667; d. 24 August, 1667.
v. Samuel, b. 18 March, 1669; d. before 1688.
⎧ Elenor, b. 11 February, 1671; d. young.
⎨ Elizabeth, b. 11 February, 1671; m. 19 June, 1707, Samuel Bur
⎩   of Charlestown; d. in 1756; he d. in 1719.
viii. Elenor, b. 15 February, 1674.   4

4. IV. ELENOR JENNER, youngest child of Thomas, born at Charlestown 15 February, 1674; married 26 October, 1701, William Wyer; died in December, 1747; he died in February, 1749.

* " Dec. 12. *Clutterbuck* arrives [from England] and brings news of Capt. Jenner's death, wido. Winsley's son." Samuel Sewall's diary.
† Of these six children three died young, and the others were:
i. Thomas, b. at Charlestown 21 December, 1693.   1
ii. Elizabeth, b. at Boston 27 July, 1696; m. 29 September, 1715, Ezekiel Cheever of Boston; d. 5 May, 1728; he d. in 1770.
iii. Abigail, b. at Boston 19 September, 1700; m. 22 September, 1719, Edward Wyer of Charlestown; he d. soon, and she m. secondly, 29 November, 1722, John Stevens of Boston; d. in 1782; he d. in 1735.
1. THOMAS JENNER, born at Charlestown 21 December, 1693; married 3 July, 1718, Joanna, daughter of Samuel Everton of Charlestown; died 23 June, 1765;‡ she died 16 May, 1771; he had twelve children, born at Charlestown, of whom seven died young; the others were :
i. Mabel, b. 23 January, 1725; m. 9 July, 1747, Rev. Samuel Bird of Dorchester and New Haven; d. soon: he d. 3 May, 1784.
ii. David, b. 20 October, 1732; Harvard College 1753; d. 1 July, 1754, drowned in crossing the ferry alone in a canoe.
iii. Joanna, b. in January, 1734; m. 1 March, 1753, Edward Carnes of Boston; d. 21 July, 1772; he d. 19 August, 1782.
iv. Samuel, b. 3 November, 1735; m. 17 July, 1757, Mary Sherrard of Boston; was of Charlestown 1771, but I know no more.
v. Abigail, b. in February, 1741; m. at Boston 1 November, 1764, David Goodwin; d. 26 May, 1811; he d. 21 January, 1825.
‡ An engraving of his tomb, with a Jenner Coat of Arms, may be seen in the HERALDIC JOURNAL for 1865.

The Trerice Family.*

Nicholas Trerice, undoubtedly of Cornish origin, was admitted an inhabitant of Charlestown in 1636; had wife Rebecca; was Captain of the "Planter," which brought many immigrants to New England in 1635; in 1648 his ship was taken at sea by Prince Charles, and carried to Holland, where it was offered to be released for £2,000, but its fate is not known; he died in 1652; she married secondly, 6 December, 1665, Thomas Lynde of Charlestown; died 8 December, 1688. Her will is printed page 32. Children:

i. Elizabeth, b. ———; m. Thomas Kemble of Charlestown and Boston; d. 19 December, 1712; he d. 29 January, 1689.
ii. Rebecca, b. in 1636.   2
iii. John, b. at Charlestown 26 May, 1639; m. 3 September, 1663, Hannah, daughter of Thomas Lynde of Charlestown, by whom he had children; he d., and she m. secondly, 12 December, 1679, James Kelling; she d. 30 December, 1690.
iv. Sarah, b. ———; m. 10 August, 1666, John Goose of Charlestown; d. in November, 1686.
v. Samuel, b. at Woburn 7 May, 1643; probably d. young.

2. II. Rebecca Trerice, probably second child of Nicholas, born in 1636; married 22 May, 1655, Thomas Jenner; died 23 September, 1722, aged 86; he died in 1686.

Katherine (Myles) Coytmore.†

Katherine Coytmore, mother of Parnel Nowell (p. 73), came to New England in 1636 or 1637, and died at Charlestown 28 November, 1659, an aged widow. She was daughter and co-heiress of Robert Miles‡ of Sutton in Suffolk; married Thomas Gray of Harwich in Essex, who died in 1607; she married secondly, at Harwich, 23 December, 1610, Rowland Coytmore of Wapping, London, who died in 1626. The wills of both her husbands are already in print. Her will is printed page 9. By her first husband she had:

i. Susan, b. at Harwich in 1593; m. Manuel Eaglesfield of London, who d. in 1625; she d. before him.
ii. Thomas, b. at Harwich in 1595; was of Wapping; d. in 1627.
iii. Robert, b. at Harwich in 1598; d. in 1598.
iv. Parnel, b. about 1602; m. ——— Parker, who d. in 1626, leaving a daughter; she m. secondly Increase Nowell; d. at Charlestown 25 March, 1687; he d. 1 November, 1655.
v. Katherine, b. about 1604; m. Thomas Graves; d. at Charlestown 21 February, 1682; he d. 31 July, 1653.

---

* See New-England Historical and Genealogical Register, XLVI, 173.
† See New-England Historical and Genealogical Register, XXXIV, 253.
‡ Alice, the other daughter and co-heiress of Robert Miles, married Thomas Wiseman of Canfield, Essex, and was ancestress of the present Sir William G. E. Wiseman, Baronet.

8

By her second husband she probably had:

i. Thomas, b. ———; m. at Wapping 24 June, 1635, Martha, daughter of William Rainsborough; d. by shipwreck 27 December, 1644; she m. secondly, in December, 1647, Gov. John Winthrop, who d. 26 March, 1649; and she m. thirdly, 10 March, 1652, John Coggan, of Boston, who d. in 1658; she d. in 1660.

ii. Elizabeth, b. ———; m. William Tyng, who d. at Boston 18 January, 1653.

Rowland Coytmore had a first wife Dorothy, daughter of ——— Lane, widow of William Harris, whom he married at Wapping 28 March, 1595, and by whom he had:

i. Elizabeth, b. in 1596; undoubtedly d. young.

ii. Sara, ———; ? m. William Rainsborough, and d. soon.

Dorothy, wife of Rowland Coytmore, had by her first husband William Harris, who died in 1592:

i. William.

ii. Samuel.

iii. Susan, b.———; m. at Wapping 24 January, 1609, William Ball.

iv. Dorothy, b. ———; m. at Wapping 27 August, 1611, Thomas Lamberton, who d. in 1627.

INDEX OF NAMES.